Not a Witch,
Not a Fairy

Also by Navita Dello

The Secret of the Ballet Book
Mimi-Marina and the Magical Doll Shop

Not a Witch, Not a Fairy

Navita Dello

To my mother,
always my rock

Chapter 1

Some figured I was a broomstick rider. Others figured I was a person of wings. In case you got it wrong too; no, I'm not a witch, not a fairy. I'm just an ordinary kid. Plain ordinary, I tell you – in spite of my name also suggesting not.

Trust Mum to call me Marvel. She said it described my recovery that voided the proposition I'd increase the infant mortality rate and left the doctors baffled. My recovery, she piled on, branded me the *miracle baby*. Okay, fair enough.

But now there was nothing marvellous, wonderful or fascinating in even my appearance. I was all limbs – giraffe-like, not model-like – which made me the tallest in my class. That got me noticed. And although I've tried convincing myself that Pinocchio's ever-growing nose was worse than mine which turned up at the tip, my nose got me noticed too. Luckily, I was hugely skinny, so I occupied less space that meant there was less of me to notice.

Anyway, what left me flustered over the years was how the *miracle* bit dropped off my radar and got replaced by labels such as *weird* and *freaky*. People are fickle, aren't they? I guess you could ask whether the situation has changed because now even the boring task of unpacking the boxes cluttering my babyhood bedroom was making me smile. The truth is I haven't been able to wipe off my smiley face since Mum told me we were leaving Moon City and moving back to her house in Crickle Town – the country town in Bluebark Valley where I was born and tagged a miracle, and where Mum and Gran also had their first peek at the world.

I slammed my palms on a box to vote hands down that what *was* marvellous was putting masses of land between me and my Moon City Primary schoolmates. No more labels to ignite the enquiry: 'Are you a witch or a fairy?'

Silly or what?

My radar now cleared, I could sniff a new start.

I went on giving my task a cheek-to-cheek ... until I

heard it. I shut my eyes, I listened. Yeah, the sound was the same as it had always been. I suppose it was too much to expect that I could also distance myself from the tune which had played in my head since I was little, the tune that was unknown to everyone else, including my flute teacher in Moon City. That's how the piece got its title: The Tune. I reckoned I'd have to live with it. No worries, I could handle that. How could I complain about music that seemed to be telling me something in time to the rhythm of gentle waves?

Yet as soon as The Tune ended, my skin went prickly because it always left me pondering whether my school-mates were right in calling me weird. It didn't help that this self-doubt made their whispers and giggles which spooked me in their absence, noisier and noisier. Not that they knew about The Tune, but the other stuff.

Before the turmoil in my head drowned me, I climbed out of the window and sprinted to the middle of the backyard. I scrunched my eyes, bunched my fists, lifted my arms to the sides and was off spinning – I'd slipped into my wishing phase. 'Please have me tagged *normal* at school. Normal ... normal ... normal ...' I've had this sneaky feeling for ages that there were forces beyond the clouds considering all our wishes. Hoping mine would be transmitted in a jiffy, I tried spinning faster. I couldn't twirl in top gear because I was weighed down with the burden of asking for that same thing over so many years.

Those memories got me wobbling to a halt. I blinked away the wetness in my eyes and glanced around the yard which had taken the toll of the summer sunshine. It was then I spotted a footpath, snaking its way through the trees that hid most of the grey stone back wall. Ooh, ripe for exploring. Wasn't that what new arrivals did? My spirits rising, I dashed to the opening in those over-grown trees. I nudged my way down the path, manhandling the unruly branches as well as the clumps of bushes nestling among the trees in a tangle. I came out all itchy at the other end.

And bang in my face stood two concrete pillars that made my tall self feel short. The pillars supported an archway carved in the back wall. I rushed at the wall and poked my head through the arch.

'Whoa!' Green fields, everywhere, green fields. How did Mum, the exercise junkie, forget there were grounds beyond?

I picked my way back as fast as the overgrowth would allow me and flew across the yard to get her. Where better for her walks? The other side of the wall was beck-oning; we had to cross over. Now.

I grabbed the kitchen door. 'Mum!'

She was there, but not alone.

'I was coming for you,' she said. 'Meet our new neighbours – Lucy and her niece, Sky. They've brought us this cherry pie, large enough for ten.'

'Oh, hello, love,' Lucy said, throwing her plump arms around me.

I had never been wrapped in the arms of a stranger. I put it down to a country-style welcome. 'I'm Marvel,' I said. 'The pie looks yum. Thanks.'

'Sky has been admiring your gorgeous backyard for years,' Lucy said, playing with the bead chain hanging from her red-rimmed spectacles. 'The people who lived here earlier didn't have kids, so she didn't get asked over as such.'

'Go on,' Mum said, gesturing at me. 'Take Sky outside and show her around.'

With my eyes off the pie and my body tangle-free, I could reflect on the girl who was doing a padding-on-air kind of move towards me. I couldn't help chucking in the *cute* word. Her moss-green eyes were full of laughs as she flicked back her long, blonde hair that was clipped back on one side with a sprig of ivory buds. What made me gulp, though, was her nose, button-like, dainty. Being my most unfortunate human part, the nose-thing, I tell you, always got me in a huff.

I had to barrel in a breath just to fire up my voice. 'Game to explore?'

'Game!' Sky said, following me out of the kitchen. She floated halfway up the yard, and now I was trailing her. She'd become the leader in my backyard.

A nerve twisted inside me; I wasn't sure whether it was because she was cute (which wasn't her fault) or from her taking over (which was her fault).

Sky's first port-of-call was the sturdy wooden frame from which hung our two-seat bench swing. 'You are lucky,' she said, perching on the bench and rocking herself with almost no movement as though she was lulling herself to sleep. 'Our garden is small. I keep telling Aunt Lucy we should sell up and get a place with a big backyard like yours.' Her eyes shifted to the spacious barbecue area by the house. 'A yard like this would be swell when my gang came over.'

Why wasn't I surprised that Sky was one of those cool kids who belonged to a gang? To make up for my unjust irritation with her, I pitched my tone to chummy and said, 'If you think this yard is great, you should see the adjoining fields.'

Sky screwed up her eyes. 'What fields?'

'That-a-way,' I said, waving at the back wall.

'That's Crickle Town Primary, except that you have to

enter the school from Cline Street – the parallel road be-hind our properties.'

I wriggled my nose. 'You're sure?'

'You bet! I've been going to that school since like Year 1. Same school?'

'Yeah, Year 6.'

'Me too. And that's where our school is.' Sky pointed in the direction I had and kept her finger there for longer than necessary.

'The archway in that back wall leads to the fields,' I said, hotting up in self-defence as if I was in a war zone. 'See for yourself!' I strode to the narrow path and scram-bled through the thicket, sensing Sky on my tail. I swished the last branch out of the way and stepped onto the gravel strip between the trees and the wall.

I stared and stared.

The backyard wall was stone solid.

No pillars.

No archway.

Chapter 2

'So, where's the arch?' Sky asked, creeping sideways alongside the wall.

'It was here a few minutes ago,' I said, dying to cover my face in case it had swapped with a beetroot.

Sky returned to where I was standing. 'Right *here*?' She tapped the wall in front of me, and then drew circles on it with her palm. She wasn't wearing the witch-or-fairy? look the crowd at Moon City Primary had pulled on. But there was something in those mossy eyes I couldn't figure.

'Bet they'll think you're odd,' Sky muttered.

'*Who?*'

'Kids,' she said. 'At school.'

At School? I bit my tongue to suppress a howl, but I

couldn't control my heart pounding. Seeing things that weren't there was a whole new story. Was my so-called weirdness spreading? Or my *oddness*, as Sky had put it? What if she told our classmates about the new girl in town and her vanishing archway?

Was I destined to relive my she's-a-freak past?

I woke up next morning with bold determination. True, I'd charged down to Cline Street after Sky left and found, as she said, that Crickle Town Primary occupied the lot where the fields had been. True, I'd spent the rest of the day trying to work out how an arch in a wall could go missing. And true, I'd sunk in a bath of sweat about going to the same school as Sky in a few days.

I still had time, today's persistent me decided, to prove to Sky there *were* fields if only the archway would appear again, crazy as that may sound. I had to stop her from blabbing about me – my life in Crickle Town depended on that.

Soon, I was out of my window and dashing through the yard despite my brain highlighting that there couldn't be two venues in one spot. I wriggled through the footpath and almost crashed into the pillars. 'Arch, I don't know how you do it, but I'm glad you're here!'

My head choked with questions, but I feasted on the

greeny grasses on the other side. I'd seen right, I'd seen right! Yet I couldn't lose my face again to a beetroot. Couldn't have my new schoolmates rebranding me weird, freaky or anything else that brought on the witch-or-fairy? enquiries. I had to check out the fields before showing Sky.

I walked through the archway, and a tiny current made my skin tingle.

How very peculiar. I rubbed my arms down, standing with my feet deep in grass and my body sweltering in the sun. *Ooosh*, it was hotter on this side. Now if that wasn't strange? Nor did it add up, given that our patchy back-yard was on the other side. Were these fields blessed with ever-green grass? I swirled, fishing for clues to the strangeness, but my surroundings gave away nothing.

Sky got me panicking, and I stamped on the grass to make certain the fields weren't shifting away beneath my feet. Then I waded through the tall grass although I could have moved to the left or right and got onto grass no higher than at home. My trekking would have been easier but sticking to the strip of long grass felt more like exploring. Surely, I'd soon bump into people who'd have all the answers. What happened, instead, was I almost fell over someone.

He was sprawled on the grass, scrawny arms thrown wide open and heels together.

He looked like a cross.

I staggered back, only to realise the boy couldn't be more than my age. Possibly younger. I inched forward again and peered at him. His eyes were shut, but his mouth was smirking, and his V-shaped chin made his face way long. Cut in points he had such a funny fringe, and the rest of his thick, nut-brown hair fell well below his ears.

Had he slept here all night? I wanted to shake him, wake him, ask him a bunch of questions. I didn't want to alarm him though, so I put on my patience cap and stood watching.

After a while the boy's nose twitched; his face also gave way to a few spasms. Then he crushed his eyes tight and opened them. He stared at the clouds. He still didn't get he had company.

'Hi there,' I said, raising my patience cap and waving at him with my fingers.

The boy sat up and did a somersault. Then he bounced to his feet, his mouth forming a toothy grin. 'Early worm!' he said.

'You too, or did you sleep here last night?'

'Didn't,' he said, giving his bony shoulders a work out.

'But if I wake early, I come here to soak in the sun.' He cartwheeled around me. 'Never seen you, yes?'

'Oh, forgot the intro, I'm Marvel.'

'This is Zylo,' he said, patting his chest. 'Or, Jester of Class 5.'

'See why you're called a jester.' I cracked up. 'You're also at Crickle Town Primary?'

'Bluebark Tree School,' Zylo said. 'No Crickle School.'

'Can't be. I've seen Crickle Town Primary here. Er, around here. I'm new to this place, and I'm starting there.'

He frowned. 'No Crickle Primary in Bluebark Woods –'

'Bluebark *Woods*? Is that one of your jester jokes then? Or, oh, I get it. That must be what this side is named. Crickle Town, where my school is, is on the other side of the wall.'

'What wall?'

'The wall that –' I stopped short because Zylo wasn't listening.

His jaw had dropped, making his face look even longer. He was gaping at me; at my ears, I think. Yeah, now he was pointing his finger at my right ear.

'I've seen your kind in my history book,' he said in a thin voice which could have been referring to a descendent from Monster Land. 'You are a Human!'

'Fully human,' I said, tickled by what again seemed

an attempted joke. 'Same as you.'

'Never!' Zylo recoiled as if I was about to grab him and make him my meal. 'Can't you see?'

I decided to go along with his unusual behaviour. 'Of course, I can *see* a boy who is around nine –'

'Ten,' Zylo shot.

'Beat you,' I said. 'I'm eleven. Okay, so, I see a human boy –'

'Not!' In spite of his baggy tee-shirt, I noticed he was trembling. He was also shuffling backwards.

'Don't go!' I cried, ranting at myself for frightening him, although I couldn't fathom how. 'I've only just got to Crickle Town and don't have any friends. I would like you to be my friend, that's all.'

Zylo allowed his feet to rest, and I saw the horror in his eyes lose its grip. 'You don't know, yes?'

'I don't,' I said, wondering what I was claiming not to know.

Zylo lifted his hands and swept back the thick strands of hair that had been covering his ears.

Despite the scorcher, I froze.

It was my turn to gape …

The tops of Zylo's long ears were pointy, pointy … like … like the bottoms of ice-cream cones.

'Oh, oh,' I managed, stifling the gasp in my breath.

'Are you an elf?'

'Never!' Zylo patted his chest again. 'We are the Tree Folk of Bluebark Woods.'

'*Tree Folk?*' My head flew around in a frenzy. Was I in another realm? 'Except for your ears, you look human even in size!' I exclaimed, seeing he came up to my shoulder in spite of my being tall for my age and a whole year older. 'Tell me – does everybody living here have ears l-like yours?'

'O'course.'

I glanced around fleetingly. 'Wh-where are they?'

Zylo stabbed the air with his fist pointing out the way. 'Warning! There in the woods you will be captured and thrown into a dungeon.'

'But why?'

'You're the enemy,' he said.

'*Me?* Your enemy? I've just met you. I want to be your friend, remember?'

'You know nothing, nothing?'

'Nothing.'

'Then Zylo tells you what's in the history book: a long time ago, Human fellows felled the Bluebark trees in the woods to build their towns. Some Tree Folk died of sad sickness once their homes went chop, chop. This part of the woods was saved because it was made invisible to

Humans. That's what Lord Grailib's great-great-great, heaps of times great, grandfather did.'

'Lord Grailib?'

'The Lord of the Woods.'

'How did his many-times-great-grandfather do it? Make the woods invisible, I mean?'

Zylo reared his ears, and they looked still longer and pointier. 'Grailib magic.'

Oh, my gosh. The current in the archway could have been leaking magic, and the ever-green grass ... 'Are you Tree Folk really magical?'

'O'course.'

'You too?'

'O'course.'

'Ooh, can you turn a soft toy into a living thing?' I asked, suddenly picturing myself having a chit-chat with Kango about the Tree Folk of Bluebark Woods.

'Not yet,' Zylo said. 'Toy to life – serious magic – senior school topic.'

My brain was now digging out stuff which was making my head foggy: Mum hadn't mentioned the fields; Sky hadn't seen them. So, the fields had to be invisible. Then w-was I a witch? A fairy? I turned icy again, and my knees went quaky. 'This place is perfectly v-visible to me,' I stuttered.

'The history book says that in those days Humans saw our woods as a land of trees with holes,' Zylo said. 'This bit that was made invisible didn't catch their eye. To see it like it is, you must have *entered* the invisible woods!'

'Oh, right.' My mind messaged him a thank-you note for producing a theory which seemingly explained my ability to see the woods.

'Get the trouble?' Zylo screeched. 'This means that if all the Humans slip into our woods somehow, they'll see it, same as you. The woods won't be *invisible* anymore!'

My mind conjured a scene of the Tree Folk and humans locked in a Robin-Hood-type battle of bows and arrows.

Zylo's face looked ducked in milk gone sour. 'You got in here by breaking Grailib magic, yes? Are you trying to steal our woods?'

'I can't do magic,' I squealed, the jitters I had about being a witch or a fairy mounting again. 'I didn't even realise I was entering a magical place! You have to believe me. You must.'

Zylo went quiet, though in a second he was hopping about, his feet on fire, like. 'But you *found* a way in!'

'I came through the archway in my backyard wall.'

'Lie, lie!' He got jumpier. 'There's no wall around here.'

'You think? You'll believe me when you see it,' I said.

'Come on, I'll show you.'

Zylo's face paled at my suggestion. 'You can't show Humans the wall with the hole-thing –'

'Promise, I won't,' I said. 'And I won't breathe a word.'

Zylo buried his hands in the pockets of his long shorts, sort of reaching for something. 'Show me,' he said.

I tracked back, keeping to the tall grass so that I didn't lose my way, and Zylo's head was bobbing beside me. I didn't dare ask him any more questions because he was whistling to himself, seemingly wanting to be left alone.

Soon enough, I saw the grey wall looming in front of me, and I peeped at him. 'Look!'

'No wall,' he said, staring ahead of him.

For a split second, I speculated: no wall, I was imagining things. I widened my eyes. The wall was there still. Wall ... wall ... But I couldn't see a start, and I couldn't see an end. Even the Great Wall of China had to be shorter. What was *this* wall?

How was I going to get home without mine?

Was I going to be stuck on this side forever?

Forgetting Zylo, I dashed forward. I sprinted, I panted until I saw what seemed to be the doorway of a doll's house embedded into this expansive wall. Now I was running a marathon, but as I drew closer, the door appeared larger and larger, and more like an archway.

Then maybe *this* was my wall. The thump in my heart mellowed and ushered in Zylo which made me pause to let him catch up with me.

'What was *that* all about? Escaping or something?' he asked.

I stretched my arm as far as it would go in the way of the arch. 'There, there the hole in the wall.'

Zylo reared his ears again. 'No wall with a hole.'

'See the pillars,' I insisted, waving my hand vertically. 'I came through the gap between those two columns to get to this side.'

'No hole, no wall. You lied. You're not my friend, you're the enemy. Lord Grailib will stick you under his mansion.' Zylo's face was now like a dark cloud that was about to rain on me. 'I hate secrets, hate secrets!' he cried, posturing for a backward-ready-to-bolt movement.

I got him by the shoulders as gently as I could. 'I'm not keeping a secret. I've told you how I got here. I *am* your friend. And I want you to be *my* friend, okay? Let's keep walking.'

The cloud on his face didn't shift, but he fixed his eyes ahead of him again and fell into step with me. The confusion in my mind, though, was crippling my legs and slowing me down. Why couldn't Zylo spot the wall? If it was doing a disappearing act, how did I see it? The time

Sky didn't see the arch, I didn't either.

At last I was standing an arm or two away from the arch, but my stomach was lurching – was this endless wall surrounding something vast? Then where was my cottagey home? How was I going to find it? And Zylo, could he ...? I pounced on him. '*Wall?*'

Zylo pulled a face.

'Then what can you see?' I yelped.

'Grass.' He stepped forward and got sucked into the air.

'Zylo? Where are you? Stop showing off your magic!'

I stood blinking.

Then he resurfaced right next to me. 'If there was a wall here, how did I go on doing cartwheels in the grass?'

'Not funny,' I said. 'Watch me going through the arch in the wall. Just watch!' Then, trampling my fear of what might be on the other side, I let my feet carry me across.

My toes dug into a gravel strip, and I stared at an alley that was fighting its way through a jumble of trees.

I was in my backyard; I was home.

My sigh could have toppled a giant. Basking in safety, I pivoted to call out to Zylo.

The wall had shrunk to the length of the backyard, but I didn't see even the trace of an archway.

I couldn't get back to Zylo.

Chapter 3

Although next morning my head was splitting with everything that puzzled me, I heaved myself out of bed to do what my heart was set on.

I had to see Zylo.

I doubted whether I'd convinced him that I was his friend and not his enemy. But was I hallucinating? The woods. The Tree Folk. The magic. Were they real? I couldn't wait to find out ... *Sorry, Mum, I can't let you in on this one; can't have you announcing to the council that there are more woods in Bluebark Valley which can be cleared for expansion.*

Mum was a town planner, after all, just as she'd been in the city before losing her job of nine years which was what got us returning to the valley, even though she felt it wouldn't be the same with Gran and Gramps passing away. Besides, I'd promised Zylo I wouldn't let on about the magical woods to anyone.

'Zylo, you haven't seen the end of me,' I mumbled. Knowing now that we humans were looked upon as the enemy, I had to hide my ears. And as my short, skimpy hair didn't do it, I'd have to go for a hat.

My gaze flitted from box to box. Where was my head-gear? I spotted a box labelled M. Miscellaneous – wasn't that the one? I dug my paws into the box: Mum's stuff. What was my Baby Book doing there? I felt a giggle coming on. Mum must have thought I'd leave it behind. That journal she'd maintained, covering the first five years of my life, hadn't interested me before. Why would it when that baby had entered childhood with a she's-a-freak sticker stamped on? So, it could be the return to my birthplace that got me sinking to the floor with a sudden urge to give the book a quick flick.

On the first page of the book was a picture of me. According to the caption it was my fifth day on Planet Earth and the day I'd been whisked home from hospital. Wrapped up like a bundle, the only bits visible were a crumpled face and a pair of slits for eyes. The next page consisted of family trees, both Mum's and Dad's. Basic facts such as height and weight were on the following page. Oh, sweet, a clipping of hair too. Silky soft. Mum had attached the cutting to the page with a tiny, pink bow. Below that she had taped in a sachet of gold particles.

The sparkling stuff made me blink. What was it? I fingered the sachet and the particles changed to another shade of gold. When I jabbed the packet again, a different gold emerged. Then I viewed the packet from several angles and the particles went on doing the same. Oh, wow. Rose gold, yellow gold, old gold, nugget gold – in fact, all the shades of gold in the universe seemed to have been blended to create this rich, vibrant colour I saw when I looked at the contents of the sachet head on. No note on this one. Mum, really? I'd have to ask her what this sachet was doing in my Baby Book. I sprang to my feet, but first to find a hat.

I scouted around the clutter for my own M box. By the time I found it, The Tune was laying it on in my head. I clapped my hands on my ears. But seriously, could that smother the usual aftermath of negative pondering and giggly noises which disturbed me? For a better way, I threw myself into unpacking the box. Bags, belts – and there they were: hats and caps. I tried them on in front of the mirror. My navy cotton hat appeared to do the best job in covering my ears. I settled for it and was going to sneak out of the window when the door burst open.

Mum traipsed in, wearing her bluey sweatpants. Her face was flushed, and she had managed to get her hair, which was no more than a boyish bob, ruffled.

'Did you go somewhere else to exercise?' I asked.

'I did, and you seem about to,' she said, eyeing the hat on my head. 'Well, I walked up the hill to test my endurance.' She gave me a broad smile. 'I'm back, aren't I? And with an invitation for you.'

'For me?'

Mum wagged her head. 'I was coming in when Lucy hailed me over the fence and asked you over for breakfast with Sky.'

'Don't want to go to Sky's.'

'Thought you were hoping to make some nice friends here – and how can you do that if you pass up the first invitation you get?'

'I mean, not this minute,' I said, although I meant *never*. Sky had probably warned her gang to be prepared for the *odd* girl joining their school.

'It will be downright rude if you don't go. And didn't you say that Sky was going to be in your class? You should be so lucky to walk into a new school feeling you've already got a friend.'

Or a blabber, or a troublemaker who'd spark a fire that would burn my chances of making a go here, I added silently, observing the corners of Mum's lips turning down. And, I tell you, they weren't going to change direction any time soon. I wrenched off my hat and hurled it, aiming at my bed. Then I stomped out of the room.

'Okay, I'll go if I must!'

Chapter 4

My heart rattled as I entered the property next door, and I knew it had nothing to do with the uneven road. The red-roofed pink house plonked in the middle of the lawn was like a cross between a danger sign and an iced cake. I affirmed at once my preference for the cottagey feel of my white home which had trelliswork bordering the roof and then skirting the top part of the pillars that supported the ceiling of our front veranda. Cosier, I decided, to comfort myself.

I tackled the steps that led to Sky's house in an ant-like manner to put off the inevitable. Then I tried taking a swipe at the wooden recliner chairs and the tiny tables that were neatly placed on their veranda. Yet it was the solitary bench, strewn with things, on my own veranda which seemed tacky. I reached for the leaf-shaped knocker and banged it as softly as I could, hoping they'd not hear me. Wouldn't that be an excuse to go home?

I wasn't that lucky.

The door opened pronto. Lucy's beaming face appeared first, and then the rest of her. 'Come in,' she said, and I had to pose for another bear hug. 'You're right on time. But mind the floor, it's just been mopped.' She ushered me into the kitchen.

Sky was perched on a stool at the breakfast bar, wearing a pair of denim shorts and a white crop top with mauve polka dots. Her blonde hair was plaited and wound round her head, and she had a teeny blue flower tucked above her ear. She greeted me with a smile that sealed the cute picture she formed. 'Hope you're hungry. Aunt Lucy's pancakes and crepes are the best.'

Sky was a natural.

I couldn't find anything out of order, except to be annoyed that she was a natural, unlike me.

We were soon tucking into the fluffiest crepes I'd tasted; they were stuffed with cubed chicken and avocado, and topped with melted cheese. A gingerbread loaf was on the bar to tempt us too. To quench our thirst, we were supplied with tall glasses of mixed-fruit juice. Lucy left us to enjoy her cooking, and I could hear her bustling around in the family area behind us.

Then for what appeared like no reason at all my body began heating. I fidgeted inside my sticky clothes. My heart was beating like a wild thing; it was making me breathless. My eyes were getting blurry, but as usual my mind was taking over by producing a round light – still faint. Oh, my gosh, something bad was about to happen.

The light in my mind was becoming bright – a reddish yellow, now flashing.

I was witnessing the kind of thing that had got others calling me weird.

Lucy was slipping ... the wall ... wall!

I pivoted on the stool and lunged at her, flinging my arms to get her by the waist. Just in time, too, to stop her from banging her head against the wall.

'Thank you, love,' Lucy said, relieving me of her weight and adjusting her spectacles which had slipped to the end of her nose. She looked frazzled. 'I could have had a nasty fall.'

'The floor not dry yet?' I asked, referring to the mopping.

Lucy bent over and glared at the tiled floor, and then at her sandals as if she was debating the culprit. She straightened up, shaking her head. I watched her trot from the room, happy I'd been able to tweak the scenario which would otherwise have put her in a hospital bed with a bandaged skull.

When I turned back to the bar, Sky was onto me. 'How did you know Aunt Lucy was going to fall?'

'Saw her,' I said, wallowing in my stupidity. How could I see what was happening behind me? Then a whole big cramp gripped my stomach because Sky's watchful eye was wearing the same expression it did when the arch went missing. Was she ridiculing me silently the way others did aloud, or what?

After that, we drifted into our own worlds, but as soon as we finished breakfast, Sky bounced off her stool. 'Want to see my bedroom?'

Glad she'd fractured the harrowing quietness, I whipped up the best smile I could and followed her to her room. It was as cute as its owner. The furniture, all in cream and peach, consisted of everything possible. There was a dressing table with drawers, a desk with a swivelling chair, a bedside table with a lamp, and a cupboard that took up almost a whole side. Even her bed had a cream base and a peach bedhead. My eyes followed the border of leaves that ran along the wall just below the ceiling, as well as halfway down. The rest of the wall had itsy specks. 'Like your wallpaper,' I said.

'Daddy put it up when I was small. Aunt Lucy says it

looks old and we should redecorate, but I don't want to. I want to keep what Daddy fixed for me.'

I picked up the framed photograph by her bedside lamp. An older version of Sky was smiling into the camera. Next to that lady was a man who seemed more than six feet tall. He was wearing a kind of turban on his head. I flinched at his long scar which began below his left eye and ran right down his cheek. 'Your parents?'

'Hmmm.' Sky's tone was lifeless.

'You've got your dad's green eyes,' I said, placing the photo back on the table.

'That's the only picture I have of them because Daddy didn't like cameras clicking.' Her face fell. 'They both died on me.'

'Oops, sorry to have raked it up. My dad died when I was six, but it must be terrible to lose both.'

'It was all *his* fault,' Sky said.

'Your dad's?'

'Daddy used to disappear frequently, and Mummy was left pining for him. He always came back, for only short spells though, as if he was visiting us. Then when I was seven, he vanished for good. That killed Mummy. I watched her dying slowly, and I tried to –' Sky swallowed the rest of her sentence. 'It was painful to watch.'

'Must have been. Way bad.'

'Then Aunt Lucy – she's Mummy's sister – took over. She was unmarried and also living in the valley at the time.'

'She's great, isn't she?'

'Swell. I couldn't have got better.' Sky's voice went wavy. 'But I miss Daddy. I was his princess. He called me Princess of the Sky.' She darted across to her desk and fished out a book from a drawer. 'See what we did to-gether!' The greenish book cover was decorated with sketches of leaves and the title at the top was *Sky's Leaf Book*. She settled into her swivelling chair. 'This is how Daddy got me to learn the alphabet.'

She began flicking the pages, and I peered over her shoulder. 'Apple … Boat … Cat,' I read, studying how those shapes had been made with pressed leaves. 'What a smart idea.'

'Daddy helped me get the pictures right, and I had to write what they were at the bottom of each page. We used to check the edges of every leaf to make certain they weren't bent before placing the leaves between the pages of a hefty book.'

The second half of the book had random leaves. 'Didn't realise a leaf came in so many types and sizes,' I said.

Sky shut the book and spun the chair to face me. 'This is my favourite thing.' Her eyes were dreamy. 'Even though Daddy was never around much, he always did stuff with me – wish it could be like then. Wish he was here to pick flowers and stick them in my hair.'

'Oh, so it was he who got you used to wearing flowers all the time.'

'You bet.' Sky grinned. 'Hey, did you find the arch in your wall? And the fields?'

I wanted to rub that grin off her face. Here was I thinking we may actually become friends, that we had crossed a bridge and come off hand in hand. No, she had to botch things. Again, she wasn't giggling or calling me names like the others. Still, she was making me crumbly.

If she thought her chipping away at me was going to weaken me into telling her about Bluebark Woods, she was mistaken. Very. My promise was to Zylo – my friend. Besides, I didn't want to be responsible for human cruelty, the sort that could result in the Tree Folk losing their lives and homes again. As much as I wanted to clash a cymbal, beat a drum and announce that the fields existed, I buttoned my lips.

Yeah, I had to forgo my chance to point out I wasn't *odd*.

Sky appeared to think my silence meant defeat. 'Behind your house is our school,' she said. 'You'll love it. The main event for this term is the class play. How was your old school? Bet you're missing your friends.'

I glanced at my watch, while mentally grabbing Sky by her hair and dangling her. She was invading every nook inside me, allowing no hiding place for private matters. 'I have to go,' I said. 'I promised Mum I'd help her with the unpacking this morning. Thanks for break-fast.' Without waiting for a response, I hurried from her room, and she followed me like a shadow.

'See you at school,' she said, waving me out.

'Will do.' School. How dare she rub it in?

Chapter 5

I got home to find that Mum had already left for work. I was glad. If she had been around I'd have told her that our button-nosed neighbour was not going to be my friend. That my visit had been a disaster. That it was *her* fault I'd started a new list of she's-a-freak fans. By having time to calm down, I'd prevent that ugly scene. Prevention was better than cure, right? The other reason I didn't want to tango with Mum was that I was still training myself to hold back about Bluebark Woods.

Of course, Kango was sitting on my bed, waiting for me as usual. My big, soft kangaroo didn't think I was weird. Come to think of it, Mum didn't either. She'd relegated my foreseeing accidents to a sixth sense. She even agreed with me that it was nonsense to call me a hero when I stopped an accident only to join the she's-a-freak club later. People are fickle, right? Then again, Mum would shake hands on whatever it took to keep me away from the loony bin.

I gave Kango a cuddle and grabbed my hat. I pulled it down on my head and peeked in the mirror. All good. My ears were well tucked in. Then I got out of the window, crossed my fingers and dashed across the yard.

At the end of the footpath, I was greeted by the archway.

I came out on the other side, enduring the sting of the arch current which made the magical exploration I was to embark on very real. A thrill surged inside me, rinsing off my lurking fear of being dumped in a dungeon. I pawed my hat. Capture-proof. Now to find Zylo: he was my friend, not Sky. I set off in the direction he had pointed.

Before long, my eyes were bulging. Branches sprouting from treetops had formed helmet-shaped canopies, making the woods look like a field of giant mushrooms. The rough and deeply furrowed bark of the tree trunks was purplish blue. Ooh, now it was easy to guess how the valley got its name.

I quickened my pace, ploughing through grass that was entertaining tiny pink flowers, which popped up here and there. Then I came to a point where the grass had been cleared to form a road. Trudging down that tree-lined street was when my heart took a leap out of my mouth.

Some of the trunks had short wooden doors and little round windows.

How cool. Were they for the Tree-Folk tots? I glanced around; the road was empty. But I stamped on the urge to peep through a window as I was supposed to be in enemy territory. I pulled my hat farther down my face and hastened, stopping only once to pick up a fallen leaf. Turning it in my palm, I noted the long, narrow blade, and the tip and the base which were both pointed. A shiver whooshed along my spine. I was holding a piece of the magical woods. Was I dabbling with magic?

Finally, the road opened into a market square which housed plenty of quaint stalls sheltered by thatched roofs.

And there they were.

The Tree Folk.

Masses of them, with long, pointy ears like Zylo's.

I stood gasping. *I* was the alien from another planet peeping in from the outside. I fumbled with my hat and, to tame my quivers, looked upon them through new eyes that focussed on their sameness to humans ...

Spotting some Tree Folk also in headgear, I entered

the square and slipped into the crowds unnoticed. Soon I was threading my way around those who were bustling with bags in their hands, bags on their shoulders and on their backs. Trading seemed rife. Browsing the stalls led me to food, clothes and everything else in between. I didn't hang around any booth for too long in case the folk got talking to me. With my head lowered, I went on checking out the wares, avoiding all eye contact until there was a hiss in my ear. I dropped the roll of ribbon I was examining and turned my neck reluctantly.

The hisser was Zylo.

In greenish long pants tucked into black boots and a matching waistcoat over his white shirt, he appeared to be wearing his Sunday best. His long hair looked polished to shine and his fringe too was well intact.

'What are you doing here?' he whispered ferociously.

'I came to meet you,' I said, holding my hand over my mouth.

Zylo glared at me and parted his lips just enough to slip one word. 'Speed!'

But we weren't quick enough.

'Zylo-boy, aren't ya going to introduce me to your friend?'

The speaker was the oldish Tree-Folk woman standing behind the counter we were at. Her pointy ears stuck out through her stiff, red hair, which was parted dead at the centre of her head. The straightness of that parting made me think of practical, sensible, no frills. Or maybe what got me going was her using even her neck for display, by wearing several strings of brightly coloured buttons.

'Grammie, I –'

'Alolla,' a Tree-Folk man interrupted to hand over a box of lace trimmings to her. He had a broad forehead, and his hair, combed neatly back, had a wet-look that made it seem jelled.

Papa, Papa, Zylo mouthed, elbowing me to move on.

I gave Alolla a half-smile and merged with the crowd. Then I tagged after Zylo who was thrusting his toe into every gap. Soon he was hailed by another Tree-Folk woman. She was poking her tattooed neck through the flock and waving at him. She looked as if she had horns because her pinky beige hair had been swept high and tied in a bun on either side of her head. I was itching to stop at her stall consisting of tiers and tiers of wooden trays packed with sweets, but of course I couldn't, because Zylo was shoving to get past and ignoring the hailer who now had her slanted eyes hooked into me.

When we got out of the square, Zylo turned on me. 'You disappeared! Knew you had powers. You are starting trouble, yes? You are bringing the Humans?'

'No, on both counts,' I returned. 'Didn't I say I want to be your friend?'

Zylo was peering at me, and I think it was my face he was reading, not my words. Then I saw the fear in his eyes dissolving.

Seeing his tension ease caused a happy flutter in my heart because I didn't mean to upset him, knowing first-hand what it was like to be harassed by others. 'Hey, who was the woman at the sweet stall?'

'Oh, Conielle. A family friend. Got the best sweetshop in the woods. She's okay, a bit nosy but.'

'So that's why she was staring at me – probably wanted to know who you were with.' Now we were down the road I was on earlier. 'I love the trees,' I said. 'The doors and windows in the trunks are the coolest. Were they fitted for the kiddies to play?'

'And to live,' Zylo said, 'with their families.'

My feet stopped walking. 'You live in a tree?'

'O'course, where else would Tree Folk live?'

'*But how?* Do you shrink to fit?'

Zylo's grin wiped away the nervy frown on his face. 'It's the other way around. The Bluebark tree broadens its trunk to make space for us inside. It doesn't show from the outside, unless you peep into the trunk through a window.'

'*Really?*' I realised then what was missing here.

Buildings.

There were none whatsoever.

'You've got to show me your home,' I begged. 'I so want to see your tree house.'

'Never!'

I tapped my hat. 'No-one will know I'm human.'

'If Grammie or Papa sniff you out there will be trouble, big trouble.'

'Everyone is at the market, right? We could nip in and out before anyone got back.'

Zylo groaned.

I kept my begging face going.

'Papa also hangs around the square on Market Day,' he muttered. Then he punched the air to his left. 'We live down Seedturf Street.'

Chapter 6

I stood in front of Zylo's tree house. It was fenced with a colourful round of flower beds that could have pulled the world out of a depression. The tree was one of the taller ones, and I had to strain my neck to see the last round window. True to his word, Zylo didn't transform us into an elf or a fairy size. Yet what if the tree didn't expand?

Zylo mumbled something, and the wooden door in the trunk grew wide and high enough for us to enter.

I clutched my sides.

Next, the magic door opened, all on its own.

Zylo disappeared into the trunk that looked dark from where I was standing. I was swamped by cold sweat, but lunged forward to follow him, anticipating a snarl from my organs.

But as soon as I stood in the doorway, I found myself breathing comfortably in a spacious, circular living room.

Oh, my gosh, this was unreal.

The ceiling of the room was panelled in wood and chairs decked with multi-coloured cushions were arranged around the reddish rug hugging the centre of the floor. What got me diving across the room and just past a small round table, hiding under a beige lacy table cloth, was the rocking chair. 'Your Grammie's seat?' I asked, eyeing some samples of ribbon by the vase of flowers on the table.

Zylo fell into one of the other chairs trembling with laughs. 'If only Grammie knew a Human was rocking in her chair.'

'Even the little window has grown!' I said, pointing at it.

'Though tree-house windows look small from the outside, because they're big from the inside, you can even climb out of them,' Zylo said.

'You're sure I won't get *stuck* half-way through?' I asked, leaping off the rocking chair to test the magic window. But my eyes were now chasing the most adorable thing.

A harp.

'What a beauty!' I darted to the instrument with the

shiny gold frame and sat on the stool beside it as if I knew how to play a harp. 'I learn the flute and it sounds grand with the harp,' I said, reflecting on a few of my CDs. 'Do you take lessons?'

Zylo shuffled up to the harp, pouting. 'O'course not.'

'It's not just a girl-thing, you know. Boys play the harp too. I have a recording of a boy around your age who won an award.'

His face went ashy. 'Grammie might come back.'

I got the feeling Zylo was eager to scrap the harp-talk. I pointed at the wooden staircase. 'I've never been up a trunk from the inside. Please, please, can we go up-stairs?'

Zylo gave me an if-you-want look. Then he conquered the steep steps in twos. I followed at a much slower pace with my fingers wrapped around the handrail, which was supported by banisters made out of log-like chunks stuck into the steps.

He entered the first room we reached. 'Zylo shows you the library-kitchen,' he said like a tour guide.

I soon saw what he meant.

On one side of the room, a huge table was cluttered with pots and pans. Odd-shaped kitchen utensils were hanging from hooks on the wall. And below them there were racks stacked with bottles of what looked like sauces, grains and seeds. On the floor were several baskets of vegies and fruit. My eyes roamed to the other half of the room where the wall was covered with semi-circular shelves housing neat rows of books. To reach them, I had to skirt past another table and some chairs set for reading. 'Books a family hobby?'

Zylo grinned and patted his chest. 'We read greedy and eat greedy.'

My mind went story books ... history books ... craft books ... until I came to a thick book that was titled, *Laws of the Land*. Oozing with wonder, I got the book out and placed it on the table with a thud. The book was covered in dust and when I flicked the pages, I found that though many of them had yellowed, not one was marked or creased. 'Hasn't this book been read?'

'Too long even for our greed!' Zylo said. 'It belonged to my great-great-grandpa.'

I glanced through the contents: Rules of the Land; Duties of the Lord; Responsibilities of the Citizens ... Picking an entry at random got me to the page headed, Rights of the Citizens. The list went on and on – The right to be protected from aliens; The right to be treated with respect; A child's right to education; A mother's right to her child ... Ooh, I could have spent hours just in this room. But after a while, realising that time was short, I gave up reading and, with the book being heavy, slotted it into the closest gap.

'Not there!' Zylo cried, pointing at an empty space farther away. 'That's where you got it from. Grammie says that Papa used to call Mama a librarian because she was fussy over how the books were kept – every book had to go back into the right place with Mama.'

'So true too, the way the books have been arranged in categories and all.' I returned the law book to its rightful home. 'Hey, I missed your mama at the market.'

Zylo went ghostlike and hung his head.

'Is your mama sick then?' I asked, wishing my mouth was stitched.

'She's dead,' he said. 'I think.'

'*You think?*' I stared at him.

'Grammie becomes all tight-lipped, and shaky, and choky, and sweaty whenever I ask her what happened to Mama. So I end up dumping the question because I can't have her getting sick or something. What if I lost her also? Papa is worse: he gets upset and locks himself in his room for days even if I talk about Mama. Grammie says that for papa, bringing up Mama is like stirring the dead.' Zylo squashed his eyes, possibly to hold back the tears as boys don't like soppy. 'Others think Mama's up to something – on a special mission maybe. O'course they could be afraid I'll end up in a nut house if I was told she was never coming back. But from the way Papa and Grammie behave, I can tell that Mama is dead. Dead, dead!'

I was in perfect synch with Zylo's frustration, and now I guess I got why he hated secrets. 'Listen,' I said, patting his shoulder. 'I know how it hurts because my dad died.'

'Mama died when I was three. Trilata –'

'What a lovely name, your mama's?'

'Mama's name was Trimoni. Trilata was my sister.'

'Oh, no, you lost your sister too?'

'Trilata was born and then went dead. It put Mama and Papa down, like into a black hole. A year later they had me. I can't remember Mama. She was a teacher at Bluebark Tree School.' Zylo pointed to a shelf of books. 'Those were hers.'

'Ooooh, did she *really* teach magic?' I asked, rolling my eyes at the titles of the guidebooks.

'O'course. And subjects like music and drama.' He jabbed his eyes again. 'You need to leave before Grammie or Papa gets home,' he said, rushing his words. Then he hurried his feet too out of the room.

I followed him down after a backward glance at the steps going up. What could be there? I didn't push for more, recognising it was time to back off, given how I felt when others wouldn't give me a break. The risk of hanging around too was again nudging me, so I folded away my curiosity and hastened only to land at the bottom of the staircase as the door opened.

Alolla walked in with the button necklaces still round her neck.

'You're back early!' Zylo squealed.

'Oh, so this is where the pair of ya got to. Why did ya leave?' Alolla split her stare between Zylo and me while waiting for a no-frills answer to her no-frills question.

I tugged at my hat, my heart thumping.

'Sorry, Grammie,' Zylo cut into the threatening silence. 'Bepa wanted to go through our act for the magic competition.'

'Same class?' Alolla's eyes were now nominating me, it looked like, to do the clarifying.

'Same magic circle,' Zylo said, jumping in to rescue me once more.

'I'll be off,' I said, before Alolla could get in another of her no-frills questions. Then I mustered a smile, despite the Robin-Hood-type battle re-entering my mind.

Zylo mumbled the door open and a black velvety cat stole in. Her round, yellow eyes looked like marbles. She lifted her tail and held her neck high, gazing at Alolla.

Alolla picked the cat and it nuzzled against her.

'Oi, Miss Fifi. You've been visiting, yes?' Zylo winked at me. 'It's not that we wanted a pet. She adopted us.'

'She strays a lot, this one,' Alolla added. 'Think she's got a special friend.' She scratched Miss Fifi behind her ear and it made her purr. 'When are ya going to tell us about the boyfriend?' Alolla cracked up.

My fear melted a smidgen because that laugh had something warm inside. I stroked Miss Fifi's head. She widened her eyes and her pupils got large. Her expression reminded me that 'Curiosity kills the cat'. The last thing I wanted was attention, but I shrugged off that worry, suddenly bold by my win.

Even cut-to-the-chase Alolla appeared to have bought into my disguise as a Tree-Folk girl.

Chapter 7

'Meet city girl turned country girl,' our class teacher announced, after her beginning of term comments.

'A few of us have already introduced ourselves to Marvel, Ms Upton,' Ava, the girl with the pigtails, said.

'Assertiveness! Now that's what I like to see.' Ms Upton's smile put some wrinkles around her eyes and mouth.

Anticipating Sky-sponsored whispers and giggles from my new classmates took the spontaneity out of my grin. But those faces were hosting me with country-style smiles. Cringing that Sky might have dobbed about the vanishing-arch mystery appeared to have been uncalled for. I twisted in my seat to present her with a thank-you nod, but she was busy meddling with her pencil case.

My next triumph came during science. Ms Upton gave us a quiz to refresh our memories before moving on to more advanced concepts. Then, seeing I was the only one who got full marks, she called me a genius. Guess what? Not a nerd-word from the others.

Was my *miracle* status making a comeback? Not that I wanted that either. Yet I wasn't going to whinge about this landing pad because anywhere was better than the spot of class freak.

At recess, I tried again to connect with Sky, but she was already strolling out of the class with three others. Clearly her gang. Did Sky think I was trouble? Too embarrassing? I swallowed, feeling my throat close. Then I followed the others and wound up in the hard playground, wishing they'd picked another place. Falling off climbing frames, swings and slides were accidents that occurred frequently in schools; I should know because I'd *enjoyed* hero-freak status in many a case at my old school. I turned my back to the brightly coloured equipment being devoured by the lower grades. Not that it would have helped. It was often suggested, and I was even beginning to believe, I had eyes behind my head.

Ava decided to be assertive again and claimed me for a chat. I succeeded in putting broken bones, sprains, cuts and bruises out of my mind. What I couldn't hold off was giving Sky sidelong squints. Was I trying to figure whether she was gossiping about me? Or was I yearning – shockingly – to be in her gang?

'Oh, that's Sky and her buddies,' Ava said, making it clear that my distraction wasn't subtle. 'They've been yapping under that tree for ages. They should carve their names on the trunk.'

'Who are they?' I asked, meaning Sky's gang.

'Sky's the pretty girl with the long plait to one side, sort of the boss. Mandy's the crinkly head. Ellie is curly crops. Clare is the one with bangs.'

I stole a peek at Sky again.

'Sky's cool,' Ava added, joining me in peeping at her. 'Everyone seems to be happy around her.'

Why didn't Sky have that effect on me? Was I so weird that her supposed charm couldn't get through to me? My mouth went desert-dry. How could I belong to what appeared the coolest gang in Year 6 when I'd never been even in a not-so-cool gang?

'They are very picky about who they allow into their gang,' Ava went on, again reading me. 'It's understandable because they never seem to squabble or anything. Our last year's class teacher named them the Happy Campers.'

'Talking about Sky and company, are we?' The girl

who was approaching us had reddish-brown eyes and a tiny mouth.

'Bea hears, sees and smells *everything* around her,' Ava whispered to me, and then her voice went flat. 'Hi, Bea.'

Bea's foxy eyes had a glint that hinted she'd discovered her prey. 'Sky's full of herself,' she said, diving for her target.

'Still, lots like her,' Ava said. 'She's popular and –'

'Charismatic,' I blurted, realising that my irritation with Sky hadn't permitted me to dwell on her good bits. While Ava and Bea argued about Sky, I glanced fleetingly at the playground, praying for recess to end. As we finally traipsed back to class, I blew red stars to the kids on the equipment for not requiring my services.

But would they tomorrow and the days after that?

I think I saw blood.

Yet, when the last bell rang, I left school, inwardly patting myself on the back for managing to avoid being called weird. Sky, however, was sneakily skirting around my peace of mind. She'd ignored me all day. If she didn't think I was good enough, I tell you, she could watch whether I cared. Who'd want to be in her gang, anyway?

'Wait for me!'

I dropped the foot I'd lifted. 'Oh, you,' I said, tuning

my voice to boredom station.

'Hunted for you after school,' Sky said.

Why didn't you do so while I was *in* school? I wanted to yell, but locked my lips. Making an enemy of Sky was a no-brainer.

'So, what did you think of Crickle Town Primary?' she went on, putting her foot out to cross the road.

All at once, I was boiling, and my heartbeat was running amok. Then my eyes went groggy just as my mind brightened with the power of a single light starting to flash.

Now I could see a car ... Sky!

I threw my arms forward and dragged her well back onto the pavement. I was on the nick of time to save Sky's leg from being driven away.

'W-where did that car come from?' she asked between gasps. Her face was peaky. 'H-how did you see it?'

'Just the buffer,' I said, not recognising my own voice.

Sky stared at me, again with her mysterious expression. I could also see she didn't believe a word I said. How could she, when the car had emerged from almost nowhere?

'Thanks,' she said, and went silent on me, as she'd done when I saved Lucy. Nor did she hear me say bye or unlatch the white wooden gate leading to my home.

I took comfort in the fact I'd saved someone from a life as a cripple. I tried, honestly, I did, not to think of the harm it had done me, what with allowing the most popular girl in my class to toy once more with the *oddness* notion. Now it would be only a matter of time before Sky alerted the rest of our class. They'd believe whatever she said. Scary.

For how much longer would my radar stay clear?

At home, I sat on my bed and buried my head in Kango. 'It could happen all over again, and this is how it starts,' I said, as if I hadn't spelled out the pattern for him before. 'First, they hail me the hero. Next, they call me the freak. Then they giggle, they whisper and ask me whether I'm a witch or a fairy.'

I looked squarely at Kango. 'You believe in me, don't you?'

His quietness tapped my heart; I'd rather he was as he was than transformed into a prattling living thing, even if magic could do it. Magic reminded me, though, that I had a friend who could also cheer me with his presence.

He had only to do a cartwheel or a somersault.

I slipped on my hat, slid out of my window and was on the way to Zylo's. The round windows of the tree houses now gave me the creeps by suddenly looking like probing eyes no better than Sky's.

When I got to Seedturf Street, my heavy heart felt easier to carry and became springy on seeing the tree house encircled by flower beds. I tiptoed up to the trunk which wasn't bulging or swelling. But when I peeped through the window in the trunk – Zylo was right, he was right! – their living room appeared just as big as it was from the inside.

Alolla was playing the harp, and Zylo was rocking in her chair watching her. I did, too, with my ear to the window pane.

I was listening to what I had heard in my head for years.

The Tune.

Chapter 8

I sat in the art room, the next day, with the weight of my body on the chair but the weight of my mind in Bluebark Woods. How did Alolla know The Tune? And why had Zylo put his arms around Alolla and buried his head in her shoulder when the music ended? I hadn't dared tap on the window and interrupt a moment like that, a moment that plainly only Zylo and Alolla could share.

After a sleepless night, my dozy brain was churning out no answers while I stared at the cups full of coloured pencils and paintbrushes occupying the middle of the long art room table. I jumped as Vera, who was sitting next to me, shoved a stack of white drawing paper under my nose. I was about to help myself to a sheet before passing on the rest when that familiar steam-hot sensation filled my body, and my heart began racing. Now my eyes were getting blurred and my vision was being redirected to my mind, which was brightening.

Then the flashing light that followed showed me Ava ... a supplies cupboard ...

Ignore it, ignore it, I hissed at myself. If I rescued Ava I'd emerge a freak in front of my new classmates, confirming whatever Sky might spring on them. I had to discard what my mind was depicting and save *myself*.

And then ...

From the topmost shelf of the cupboard, a large plastic storage box crammed with stuff was crashing down, and I was pulling Ava away from it just in time to spare her head from having to swap with a squashed tomato.

Miss Nesbith, the art teacher, rushed forward holding out her arms. 'Are you all right?'

'Yes, Miss,' Ava said, brushing herself down and neatening her pigtails. 'I didn't see that coming – oh, Marvel, *thank you*.' Her eyes were saying, *You are a hero*.

'Who on earth put that hefty box up there? Was it anyone from this class?' Miss Nesbith's deep-set eyes bulged in her attempt to spot the offender.

While the denials of wrongdoing went on, Bea, who had marshalled herself to the accident scene, beamed a cunning glint at me that said, *I love to stir*. 'How did you see the box coming down?' she asked.

Now I was her prey.

'Er,' I stuttered. 'I must have –'

'You weren't turned that way, were you?' Bea's eyes were foxier than ever.

'She couldn't have been, because I was passing her the paper pile,' Vera said, joining us by the cupboard, her face netted with confusion.

I stooped, hoping I'd shrink till I got lost inside my shoes. 'D-don't recall exactly –'

'Same as yesterday! After school when I saw you dragging Sky off the road, I wondered how you spotted that car,' Vera said. 'I was just behind you two but didn't even hear it. You, you must be a good fairy.'

'Or a good witch,' Bea added, clearly to spice things up. Then she flashed her glint at the others. 'Class, we've been gifted with a good witch or fairy in disguise.'

The first giggle hit my eardrums.

I began running out of oxygen.

Then a second giggle.

A third.

I was gasping for air, and lost count ...

'Quiet, everybody!' Miss Nesbith shooed us back to our seats. Then she pushed the box into the space she'd made on the bottom shelf of the cupboard. She straight-ened up, seemingly vexed. 'What a blessing no-one was hurt and the box didn't open. Well, all of you, please make sure you put things away sensibly at the end of each class.'

After art, we traipsed back to our classroom, me with my eyes and ears to the ground. Luckily, Ms Upton was already there and eager to begin our English lesson. Soon the class was immersed in several newspaper texts reporting the same event. Then the silence was suddenly broken by a crash and a thud, followed by a screech from Mandy.

Her pile of folders was strewn on the floor.

'Mandy, can we have less noise?' Ms Upton asked with false politeness.

'The files moved along my desk and fell over, Miss,' Mandy yelped.

The class hooted with laughter.

'Mandy, that's enough.' Ms Upton frowned, adding to the wrinkle-count on her face.

'It must be true,' Clare butted in, giving her bangs a flick, revealing puzzled eyes. 'When I looked up for a tick a minute ago, it seemed odd that my pen which I'd parked next to my pencil on the left side of my desk had shifted to the right.' She waved a black biro. 'I kept mum because I thought I might have moved it myself, but I don't think so.'

'You didn't have anything to do with the walkabouts, did you?' Bea was smiling at me with her bitsy mouth pursed.

'Me?' I asked lamely, drawing giggles again and whispers from the others. Those noises panicked me into letting my gaze fly round the class.

And my fat error was rewarded with some witch-or-fairy? looks.

I felt the school bus drive over me.

I threw Sky a glance, possibly because my mental state was making me do irrational things or as the victims – crinkly-haired Mandy and *bangso* Clare – belonged to her precious gang. Deluded I was if I expected Sky to show an interest. Again, she'd slipped off to someplace else. What was *wrong* with her?

I recovered my glance only to find Bea in my face, still goading me with her meanie-mouthed smile. 'You're *sure*, you're sure, you hadn't just a morsel to do with any of this?'

The giggling and whispering got fierce.

I ached as if I was road to the peak-hour traffic.

'Finish your reading!' Ms Upton thundered. 'We have to discuss how the news articles differ based on their purpose and audience ...'

I didn't hear the rest of what Ms Upton was saying because my ears were still plugged into the giggle-a-whisper-thon that had left me flattened. Nor did I see the words in the article on my desk, as my eyes wouldn't let me drop the witch-or-fairy? looks I'd caught. Now weird things *were* happening, and they weren't my doing.

The rest of the class thought they were.

Was this punishment for my moment of weakness? My shameful contemplation of not rescuing Ava? I'd never entertained such a notion before. Not ever. I spluttered in stifling the tide of sobs rising inside me. But I couldn't stop myself from sinking in guilt. What was happening to me? What was I becoming?

Where was my fresh start to school?

Chapter 9

In the afternoon, I sat in the kitchen digging the table with my elbows and resting my face in my palms. My moping had to do with more than the volcano threatening to erupt at school.

The arch was also up to its old trick.

Toing and froing between the kitchen and back wall since I got home from school had not granted me passage to Bluebark Woods – the very place I had finally heard The Tune *outside* of my head.

For the billionth time, I battled with the same question: how was The Tune known in a magical place? The heat from my cheeks warmed my palms. Yeah, a magical place?

How?

I knew now that the only way to learn about The Tune was to cross over to the other side.

Except I couldn't.

Next morning, I woke with a dull headache. The one sparkle in my cloudy head was that it was Saturday. No school. I threw open my bedroom window and gazed into the distance as if the arch was going to rise above the treetops in the form of a rainbow and announce its return.

Didn't happen.

But at the wall, I got lucky.

I headed to Zylo's tree house, trying to whistle The Tune. It sounded disjointed with my erratic breathing. My body was a mess too, turned inside-out and upside-down in a way no-one would get unless they had been on the same page.

I was about to get to the bottom of what I had wanted to know all my life.

Before I reached the tree, Zylo popped out. 'Saw you,' he said, jumping over a flowerbed. 'Grammie will be back soon. You won't stay for long, yes?'

'I won't,' I said. 'I came for an answer to one big question.'

Zylo did a backflip and mumbled the door magic.

'I don't have to come in if that makes you anxious,' I said, trying again not to force myself on him.

'You don't seem like the enemy,' he said.

'Sure, you don't mind? Really sure?'

Zylo gave me a reassuring smile and nodded me in.

As soon as the magic door closed behind us, I became all gushy. 'The other day I came here to meet you, and through the window saw you watching Alolla playing the harp.'

'Good you didn't come in. If you keep knocking into Grammie, she will see through your hat.'

'The tune she was playing –'

'Grammie is the harpist, told you, not me. Yes? Yes?' Zylo sounded as though he was hunting for my question.

'What,' I asked, 'was that tune? I've, er, heard it before.'

Zylo shook his head sideways. 'It has been played in Bluebark Woods only.'

'Can't be.'

'Mama wrote that tune –'

'Your *mama*?'

'Mama. So, no-one in the Valley of Humans could have heard it.'

'I have,' I insisted, my head swimming. 'For years and years and years.'

Zylo had to be doing his rearing-the-ears thing, as I could see the tops of his ears sticking out through his long, thick hair. 'You're making a mistake, got to be another tune.' He dashed to the harp and strummed it tenderly with his head against the frame. 'This harp was Mama's. She made a book full of pieces. Grammie plays them to be with her. And when I watch, I'm with Mama too. That piece you saw me listening to was Mama's best.'

The exchange I'd witnessed between Alolla and Zylo when the piece ended, now made sense, but it still didn't leave me in any doubt that Trimoni's composition was The Tune. And that certainty stabbed my heart. How could I not recognise what had haunted me since I was little? 'What was that piece about?' I asked, hardly hearing myself.

But Zylo heard.

'The gift of life.'

Chapter 10

'You must show me your mama's book of music,' I cried, dying to get my hands on anything that might beam a torch on my life-long search.

'Not got it.'

'What if I became a renowned flutist one day and made your mama's tunes famous by playing them with a harpist?' I asked, pushing my luck. 'Grand, yeah?'

'Grammie put the book away.' Zylo was clearly not buying into my proposition.

'You *must* know where?'

'Do not!'

But I noticed where his eyes went. 'Is it upstairs?'

'Not,' he said, yet moved himself to the bottom of the staircase and stood with his feet apart.

The time had come to plead.

'Zylo,' I said, 'have you ever wondered about something? All your life? I mean a matter that affected you so much it turned your body inside-out and upside-down?'

He gummed his lips together but nodded a slow yes.

I seemed to have trodden on the loss of his mother. Ouch, clumsy me. 'This might be my only chance,' I said quietly, 'to get to the music I've been looking for since I was small. That tune has been a huge part of my life, even gets me worrying about myself. It, it might also be *telling* me something.'

Zylo sucked his lower lip. 'You are serious, yes? You can't know this tune but another piece like it, maybe?'

'Maybe,' I said, to appease him.

'Zylo will let you see it.' He turned to the staircase, and I was right behind him.

We didn't get any farther.

Orders to halt were delivered by the sound of tapping and a woman's face in the window.

'Conielle!' Zylo exclaimed.

I could barely recognise her from the market square as her pinkish hair had turned into purple streaks, and her horns had gone.

'Keep your mouth shut down,' Zylo said, before mumbling her in.

Conielle sauntered through in a long, flowing gown, carrying a heart-shaped box tied with red satiny tape. Her slanted eyes got me again, making me fidget with my hat to ensure my ears were well hidden.

Then she was all smiles for Zylo. 'Do I get to greet your friend?'

'Bepa from my magic circle,' he offered.

'Hello there, Bepa. Working together, are we?'

'Magic competition,' Zylo replied on my behalf as usual.

Conielle twisted her tattooed neck, which I now saw had a twig design. 'Where's Alolla?'

'Grammie is out visiting.'

'Rin?'

'Don't know where Papa is.'

'Tell Rin we are expecting him at the Halipac Magic Festival meeting tonight. Put a smile on his face with these, will you?' Conielle passed the box to Zylo and gutted the room with the sound of a laughing hyena. 'Your favourite Jacko candy and my latest Nutty-Choco-Fudge delights.'

Zylo beamed. 'Thanks a chunk.'

'Got to go, lovely.' Conielle ruffled his hair.

He immediately lost the smile on his face. And when she left, a load of air escaped his lips.

'She seems to be awfully fond of your family,' I said.

Zylo shrugged. 'O'course, she always gives us a bite of her new sweets for free.' He produced a roguish smile. 'I think she is after Papa. But Papa has never gotten over Mama. He doesn't laugh anymore – don't think these sweets will do it!' Zylo placed the box on the round table next to the rocking chair. 'Even Miss Fifi tries to cheer him with her snuggles. Doesn't work with Papa.'

'The music, the music,' I blurted, suddenly dwelling on the possibility of Zylo changing his mind.

He leapt across the living room and landed at the base of the steps again.

'Jester of Class 5!' I chuckled. Zylo had a canny way of plucking me off a slippery slope. Then past the library-kitchen we wound our way until we came to a landing which led to another flight of stairs that was steeper. 'How much farther?' I asked, hassled by the fear that the music book would run out on me if I took too long.

'We have to get to the magic room,' Zylo explained. 'And all the Tree Folk choose the top room of their tree house for making magic because higher up the trunk is where the tree magic is the strongest.'

I tapped the trunk wall. 'A tree seeping magic. How unreal.'

'It's not just the trunk. Every part of the Bluebark tree carries magic.'

'Like?'

'Wearing the leaves gets you leadership and prosperity. The roots are good for strength and courage ... The flowers – they can be crushed and put into medicine to squash pain.' Zylo fiddled with his pockets. 'Acorns are lucky. There's heaps more, Grammie is the one who knows. And a lot of the tree parts are used in potions.'

I stiffened with awe. 'I'm really in the midst of magic, aren't I?'

'Grammie,' he hissed, and in my head a clock ticked.

We recommenced our upward journey. When we got to the topmost door, Zylo mumbled for longer than usual with his eyes closed. Then he opened them, and with his index finger, drew a sign on that door.

It sprang open, and the room inside looked much larger than the living area downstairs. For the trunk to expand so much, this *had* to be a magical room. Before I could get in on my feet, I was swung across the threshold by what felt like a gush of air.

My eyes flew to the centre of the room which had been marked off by a huge chalk circle. Six dome-shaped lamps surrounded it. 'What's that?' I asked, striding towards the circle.

'Don't step into it!' Zylo squealed, bounding to keep up with me.

I stalled at the edge of the chalk boundary and saw that there were two steps down to a circular pit. I stared at the symbols drawn on the ground inside the pit, but it was like trying to read an ancient language that didn't own words. 'What are those signs?'

'They belong to the faraway folk we can get in touch with.'

'You *can*? Who are they?'

'We enter this speak-o-port to talk with the Tree Folk living in different places and other magical beings in certain realms.'

'Show me how it works!' I said, almost falling into the pit.

'We can't contact them for nothing – it's against the law and doesn't work. Big, ugly things can happen by trying to connect for fun.'

I recoiled, but caught up in the aura of magic, my eyes flitted around the room, and past some cabinets and low tables of curiosities before getting stuck on a row of dark cavities in the trunk wall. They looked like the portholes in a ship, and I pointed at them. 'Those?'

'To store spell books.' Zylo darted to the holes, this time making me dash after him. 'Some books have recipes for potions and things,' he said when we reached the cavities. 'There are also a few books that can never be replaced –'

'Like the music book? The music book?'

Zylo was already poking his head into a cavity which lit instantly, uncurtaining several shelves of books. My heart hammered as I watched him pull out a book with a silvery cover. It had a round crest at the top depicting a Bluebark tree and right below it was the title.

Trimoni's Music for the Harp.

Zylo placed the book in my hands, and my palms turned clammy. I opened it with a struggle because my fingers had now gone numb. He probably spotted I was needy and took over the page flick. And there at the top of the page he stopped at was the name of the piece.

Life.

That little word built a storm inside me. I braved it and pored over the music written with thin, long strokes. Hungrily, I ran my finger through each note on every line of every page of the tune.

Then the storm broke and I burst into tears.

'I don't think Mama meant for anyone to cry.' Zylo sounded alarmed. 'You are sad, yes?'

I stared at him through my tears, saddened by being far, though near – I had The Tune in the palms of my hands, but it hadn't given me a hint as to how it got into my *head. My* head.

For a moment, I pressed the open book to my chest. Then I closed it with trembling hands and returned it to Zylo.

What The Tune, er, *Life* might be conveying to me would remain buried inside that book forever.

Zylo peered into my eyes and in his I saw that he was hurting too. 'Not the music you heard, yes? Told you that Humans can't know this tune. Even if Mama *was* here, she'd tell you that *Life* was Tree-Folk music.'

Chapter 11

On the way out, we walked past the tables of curiosities I had noticed earlier, but I was in no mood to dwell on them. What won my attention a decimal, though, was a cabinet which had stuff that looked like beakers, test tubes and things. For a moment, I tried to find the link between my pet subject, science, and magic, and stumbled on the root of a giggle that strangely blossomed from inside my sorrow. 'A minute,' I said, stopping to examine the rest of the equipment that seemed to be my only anchor to sanity.

'Grammie, Grammie.'

'Okay, I get it, I get it.' My eyes quickly travelled to the upper shelves of that cabinet. On top were small glass bottles of liquid, labelled potions and serums. Below were bigger bottles, some stout, some tall, filled with vivid colour. 'Orange, blue, burgundy, green – ooh, is that magic dust?' I asked, wondering whether a sprinkle of it could make me fly.

'Dust made of wood,' Zylo said. 'I don't have a super-power colour yet. When my magic skills improve, I will know what colour to use to get best results.'

'Hey, you're running short of the gold,' I said, pointing at the only bottle which was no more than one-third full.

'Don't need that dust! Not anymore.' His voice was tight. 'That gold was Mama's super-power colour. Grammie said that only Mama knew what ingredients to mix to make that gold.'

'It's awesome: rich, shiny ... vibrant –' I jerked forward, knocking my nose on the glass door. I shifted my eyeballs slowly one way, and then slowly the other, watching the colour changing in shades. Then I moved my head around too.

Rose gold, yellow gold, old gold ...

How odd. These colour variations were the same as what I'd observed in the particles in my Baby Book. 'Can you get me that bottle of gold dust for a second?' I asked, my pulse see-sawing.

'Not allowed.'

'Please. Please.'

Zylo wrung his hands. 'Haven't been given the magic to those doors yet.'

'Oh, what?' I screeched unfairly. Then I plugged my palms to the glass door and stared at the bottle head on, keeping my eyes dead still. The colour of the dust stopped shifting too and was again sparkly, vivid ... *vibrant*.

The magic dust in the bottle appeared to be the same shade of gold as the particles in my Baby Book.

When I got home and found no-one, I remembered Mum was attending a seminar at the regional council in Preston Hill, the biggest town in Bluebark Valley. She'd said she would be returning late because the event was followed by dinner. Oops, another thing I'd forgotten. Mum had arranged for me to go to Lucy's place in the evening, insisting I couldn't be left on my own. *As if.* What made it slightly palatable, though, was that Sky was going to be away at Ellie's sleepover. So my main frustration really was that I hadn't got down to asking Mum about the contents of the sachet and why it was in my Baby Book.

And now I was tearing myself apart not knowing.

I dashed into my room and opened the Baby Book

which was languishing on an unopened box. Then I removed the tape that held down the sachet to the page and picked up the tiny packet. I blinked at the richness of the gold. Oh, my gosh, the contents *did* look like Trimoni's magic dust. I shook the sachet again and again, and the particles kept changing colour. Next, I held up the sachet and went on moving my head around it, eyeing the stuff from different angles as I had done with the gold dust. The colour kept wavering as before – and yeah, yeah, in the same shades of gold the dust had displayed.

I slipped the sachet into the Baby Book, without even taping it back to the page. Finding the source of The Tune in Zylo's magic room was mindboggling enough; oh, wait, was that why my mind was trying to make connections to things in that room? The right colour didn't indicate that the particles were magic dust. They could be something as simple as gold glitter bought from a shop. Then again, was I unravelling a pattern? A pattern that kept leading back to Trimoni? Trimoni and me. No, that didn't make sense either.

To save myself from lunacy, I restricted my thoughts and efforts to the boxes waiting to be emptied. After a while I loosened up a little, seeing my room taking shape. Nothing like Sky's. At least it didn't seem like a storeroom any longer. Before going to Lucy's, I couldn't help revisiting my Baby Book. I didn't get beyond testing the particles repeatedly.

I could very well have been staring at Trimoni's gold magic dust.

I *had* to speak to Mum.

'We're going to be in limbo as long as the kitchen is in boxes,' Mum said next morning. 'So gobble fast and let's be done with the unpacking.'

I made my mouth feel as pouty as possible. 'Sad Sunday! Except you're right. Couldn't talk much last night with you so late coming for me. Anyway, how was your seminar?' I asked, not wanting to appear too eager about the sachet.

'Pretty good. But a lot of planning to get done with the proposed project.'

'Expansion plans?' My mind was swamped with images again of the Tree Folk and humans in a Robin-Hood-style battle. 'Surely, there's no space for more towns in Bluebark Valley?'

'Oh, no, not towns. The Bluebark Highway – and land has already been allocated for it. It's the budgets, scheduling and all that stuff which still need working on. Being a long-term project, we have to get it going with minimum disturbance to the neighbouring towns and traffic flow.' Mum appeared thoughtful. 'Apart from that, planning nowadays is not just about community needs and economic sustainability. It's also about balancing development and environmental issues.'

'A good thing too.' Seeing Bluebark Woods safe sent me in a direction I hadn't set out. 'But weren't the woods in the valley cleared to build the towns?'

'The woods? Oh, I see you've been reading. Yes, that's right.' She made a funny face. 'According to legend, there were forest people, erm, magical creatures in those woods.'

I altered route immediately. 'Mum, while I was unpacking some boxes yesterday, I came across my Baby Book and gave it a flick.'

'Good for you! Thought it didn't grab you?'

'Yeah, but I was bored stiff. Anyhow, what was that sachet of gold particles next to my clipping of hair?'

Mum put down the packet of sugar she was emptying into a container. 'Strange you should ask,' she said. 'I'd forgotten that little mystery.'

My heart took a shot at the ceiling; so there *was* a mystery. 'Like what?'

'Well, your dad thought the wind had blown those powdery bits into your room. But that shining powder on your windowsill looked so alive. It was almost talking to me.'

'Talking?' I asked, reflecting on how I felt The Tune was communicating something to me.

'Yes! So, I gathered the powder and put it into a sachet instead of throwing it out,' she continued. 'Later, I pasted it in your Baby Book.'

My mind was panting. 'What did those particles, er, powder have to do with *me*?'

'Possibly nothing.'

'Oh,' I said simply, trying to sound unperturbed even as my stomach was behaving as if I'd been dropped from a cliff.

'But what really got me stashing away the powder inside your Baby Book,' Mum said, 'was that I found it on the morning after the night you had your miraculous recovery.'

'What?' I almost yelled.

'That's exactly how I reacted. Your dad said I was trying too hard to find meaning to the crisis. Considering the doctors came up with no explanation for your sudden change of condition, can you blame me?'

I barely knew where I was with my mind backtracking to the pattern I'd noticed earlier, only more clearly. It was fuelling my head with a gamut of questions: if that stuff in the sachet was Trimoni's magic dust, how did it end up in my bedroom? Did it have anything to do with my recovery? And how did Trimoni's harp music get into my head?

Trimoni? Trimoni?

What did Trimoni have to do with me?

I didn't expect Zylo to have the answers. If only Trimoni herself had been around! Then I was struck on the head with an idea.

I'd ask someone else who might know.

Alolla.

Chapter 12

I hung around till I had chucked out three empty boxes. 'Mum, I need a stretch. I'm going for a walk.'

'Okeydokey. But get back soon, we're not done.'

'Slave driver!' I said, and flew from the kitchen.

Soon I was trudging back from the wall.

I spent the rest of the day as I had a few afternoons ago, traipsing in and out of the kitchen at regular intervals to check on the wall. The arch had well and truly gone. Sticking around for it all day was like waiting for a verdict that could put me away till I was grey. Again, I was fretting – what if I couldn't get back to Bluebark Woods?

I'd never have the answers to the questions jostling in my head.

I'd live in darkness; my day would be night.

By evening I was like a caged animal snarling for grub, so I decided to scout around the area to familiarise my-self with Crickle Town.

I got to the high street where most of the shops and buzz were, and walked along the red brick pavement noting what was available. A hairdresser, bookshop, music store, general store. Then a supermarket, bank, recreation centre – oh, great, with supposedly a big pool. Also, there was a sports club with tennis courts. The Crickle Town Library came after that and then a chemist, a post office and the like which took me as far as a pavement-matching red brick town hall.

I crossed the road and landed by the clock tower that appeared to form the main feature of the town centre. Even that I didn't remember, being two when I left the valley and coming back only that once at four to visit Gran who was breathing her last. I walked on, suddenly feeling hungry, possibly because people were sitting out-side cafes having a bite. With dinner on my mind, I has-tened alongside a park. A large board informed me that the place was called the Martha Marks Park, and a banner above the board advertised a concert there next weekend. I sighed. If only I had friends to go to it with.

Now I could see little ones playing on the equipment and mums sitting around on benches. Then it happened.

I was sweating, piggy-like; I was gasping. My eyes were growing foggy. But in my increasingly illuminated mind I was seeing a wee boy running ... a swing ... up, down ... In a trice, I was over the low fence and sprinting across to the kid. I grabbed him just as he was about to take the fatal step forward into the oncoming swing.

A woman dashed to us. 'Thank you, thank you,' she said at the top of her voice to be heard above the child who'd started bawling as if he was exercising his lungs. She bundled the boy in her arms and kissed the top of his crown. 'You saved my son!' She gazed at me with that you-are-a-hero expression in her eyes.

I noticed similar glances from the others who'd surrounded us. I felt like their sunshine – until I spotted a pair of foxy eyes.

'The good witch in disguise strikes again!' Bea bellowed in spite of her small mouth.

And the crowd shrieked with laughter.

All in a tick, Bea was Miss Hero, and I was Miss Freak.

I left the park, a rain cloud. I recalled saving another kid at a park in Moon City from falling into a duck pond. But I had never got a witch-or-fairy? reaction from one-off audiences in the city. The fiascos, I tell you, had always been at places like school where the mob that witnessed my feats was always the same. In a small country town like this, it appeared that everyone popped up everywhere.

With this country town syndrome, my troubles were going to get bigger.

I could become *everyone's* witch or fairy.

It could have been Bea's absence from school the next day which allowed my boldness urge to surge, at least, when I got home. I threw on my red A-line skirt because of its deep pocket and into it carefully tucked the sachet of gold particles from my Baby Book. Then, hat on my head, I was out of my window and across yard. And like a monument that had never ceased to exist, there was the archway.

I lavished it with a smile and was soon on my way to Seedturf Street, despite Zylo's warning to keep away from Alolla. I winced whenever my bold spirit frayed and leaked pictures of me withering away in a dungeon – never to return home.

And each time my mind went, *Turn? Bolt?*

At the tree house, I peeked in on Miss Fifi snooping around while Alolla, wrapped in a robe, dozed in her rocking chair. I was gripped again by a scoot-while-you-can hysteria. It didn't last long, because boldness grabbed me by the cuff and dragged me to the door which opened when I knocked.

'Zylo!' I stammered, now standing in their doorway immersed in guilt. 'Didn't spot you through the window –'

'Grammie,' he whispered.

'Saw her,' I said. 'It's she I've come to meet.'

The tips of Zylo's ears were now showing. 'Grammie will get you're a Human!'

'Zylo-boy, who are ya speaking to?'

'No-one, Grammie, it's just –'

Driven by years of living with the unknown, I pushed my foot forward, making Zylo glare.

'Oh, your magic-circle friend.' Alolla was craning her neck and beaming at me. 'Come in, come in, don't feel shy. Any friend of my grandson is a friend of mine.'

I slipped past Zylo, who still wore his glare.

Alolla rubbed her eyes and settled back into the rocking chair. 'Zylo-boy, where are your manners? Why are ya standing there popeyed instead of asking your guest to sit?'

'We are not staying –' he started.

'Actually,' I said, raising my tone a notch, 'I'm here to see your grammie.'

'What a kind heart, time for the old –'

'We're in a hurry, Grammie.'

'I wanted to ask you something,' I said, playing deaf with Zylo and plonking myself on the chair right in front of Alolla. The rigid centre parting on her red head was now in my face, and it made me shift in my seat.

'Ah!' Alolla went on rocking in her chair. 'When is the competition? What magic trick are ya having trouble with?'

'Really, it's about the tune you played on the harp the other day.'

'Bepa, we'll be late!'

'Oh, were ya here?'

'Yeah, but didn't come in because I didn't want to disturb you.'

'Erm, now which tune was it that I played?'

'*Life*,' I said.

'So ya love it?' Alolla's eyes glistened with tears and her centre parting suddenly looked curvy. 'You should have heard my d-daughter, Trimoni, p-playing it. I still see her the day that piece won her the medal. In a long, white gown ... a garland of white flowers running down her plait of shiny golden hair ... Can ya believe it? When she sat to perform her hair reached the ground.'

Miss Fifi lured her way onto Alolla's lap as if she was clawing for praise too.

'Ya wouldn't have been more than an infant,' Alolla went on.

'But I have heard that tune before –'

Zylo binged on coughing.

'Stop your funny act, boy. We have a guest.'

'I mean, I had heard that tune *way* before I listened to you playing it,' I said, in spite of Zylo's interruptions being a constant reminder of the dungeons, and putting a dent again in my boldness.

Alolla grunted. 'Apart from that once at the concert, Trimoni didn't play *Life* for others because it was a tune she wrote for a personal reason. No-one else knows the notes of that piece except me. Must have been another tune ya heard.'

'I'm sure it was the same –'

'Bepa!'

I could hear the fluster in Zylo's voice and sense his eyes trying to meet mine.

'*Where* did ya hear it?'

I tapped the sides of my head with my hands. 'I've been hearing that tune in my brain since I was little, almost a baby.'

Alolla stopped rocking and bent forward in her chair. '*Baby?*'

'Yeah, I –'

She shut her eyes, appearing to have heard enough, and began muttering. 'Baby, baby, baby …'

Her reaction fixed the dent in my boldness. I curbed my breath and waited till she opened her eyes, and then reached into my pocket for the sachet of gold particles.

Alolla snatched one look at the sachet and put Miss Fifi down on the floor with a chug, making the cat growl. 'That's Trimoni's magic dust!'

'*Mama's? Mama's?*' Zylo squealed.

And did I see a shadow cross Miss Fifi's yellowy eyes?

'Nobody has her recipe, not even me. So that can't belong to your ma or pa. And children your age don't have a super-power colour.' Alolla's voice could have axed the tree house. '*How did ya get that dust?*'

That centre parting couldn't stop me now. Nor could the dungeons. 'This packet of dust was pasted into my Baby Book – er, the record book my mum kept of the first five years of my life.'

I pulled off my hat and chucked my hair behind my ears.

Zylo sounded as if he was choking on a boulder.

I think I even heard Miss Fifi growl again.

Alolla leapt to her feet and flapped a crooked finger at me. 'You're not one of us. You're a Human!' She grabbed me by my shoulders and yanked me off the chair.

'Grammie!' Zylo dragged her away from me. 'Bepa, I mean Marvel, is safe. She is not our enemy. She is my friend.'

In spite of the battle of arrows I had entered, hearing Zylo call me his friend sounded the declaration of an amnesty. My eyes felt teary.

Alolla's hands landed on my shoulders again. At least she wasn't gripping me; she was staring at me with hungry eyes, eyes hungry for answers. 'How did your *ma* get that magic dust?'

'She spotted the dust on my bedroom windowsill – the window I usually climb out of to get here.'

'To get here?' Alolla's hands went limp on my shoulders, and then dropped to her sides. She went on babbling, and I couldn't catch a word she was saying. 'That window must be along the Pathway,' she finally whispered. 'Ya found the Pathway Trimoni created in entering the Valley of Humans.'

Chapter 13

'Mama, Mama! Mama made a *path* to get to the Humans?'

'Why did Trimoni create a Pathway from the woods to my *bedroom*?' I threw in.

Neither of us got any answers because Alolla's lips were trembling.

'Grammie, sit – you'll fall!'

But unwilling to succumb to her wobbling legs, Alolla stood. 'Ya must be ...'

'*I ... must ... be?*' I prodded, every nano-second of her silence sucking the blood out of me. What was so difficult to say?

Alolla was grabbing me with her eyes now. 'How old are ya?'

'Eleven,' I said, my mind screaming, *What does my age have to do with it?*

She patted her mouth. 'Born 27 October?'

My skin broke out in a rash. 'H-how did you know my birthday?'

'Tell me what happened when ya were born.'

Alolla was back to her no-frills questions, and I wanted to stomp around and bang my head till I got answers. Instead, I went into lockdown and said, 'Nothing, short of nearly dying.'

With an ear-wrenching gasp, Alolla flung her arms around me. 'Trilata, Trilata, my granddaughter, Trilata.' She fell back into the rocking chair, weeping.

I stood like an iceberg, braving the rough seas. With my lips frozen, I couldn't shriek that I hadn't been adopted by my parents. Mum would have told me. Surely, she would have? Wouldn't she? Wouldn't she? And impossible, impossible – how could she have ended up with a Tree-Folk baby? Oh, my gosh. Did Mum, the budding town planner, know about the invisible woods?

'Leave Grammie alone!' Zylo's bellowing whisper severed my thoughts. 'Can't you see she is upset that a Human has entered our woods? She can't even think straight. How can my dead sister be you? You are a Human. You're driving Grammie batty –'

'Ya didn't die, Trilata,' Alolla said, rocking herself slowly. 'Ya didn't die – not completely.'

'See what you've done! You've scared her, muddled her, made her sick. I won't have a Grammie!'

At his outburst Miss Fifi jumped onto Alolla's lap, but turned her head and gave me a marbly look.

Alolla snuggled Miss Fifi and stared at Zylo, and then lingered on me for a while. 'I'm not confused,' she said. 'Better be seated – I've got a long story to tell ya.'

Was I not *me* then? I glanced at Zylo and saw that he was a mess just as I was. Then I was thrown into a chair by an explosion within me on hearing Alolla clearing her throat to speak.

'When Trilata was born, she was dying,' Alolla said. 'The only way Trimoni could make at least a part of her baby live on was by infusing the drops of her infant's energy into a third-generation Human valley girl – the baby girl had to be dying too so that Trilata's energy would be put to good use to cure the Human baby. She had to be born on the same day and at the same time as Trilata.'

'Me?' I asked.

Alolla's nod told me it was.

'How did Trimoni find me?' I cried. 'The Internet?'

Alolla frowned, and I realised that the World-Wide-

Web hadn't invaded the Tree Folk's realm.

'Trimoni fell into a trance and spotted ya fitting into all the conditions. So she crept into your house at night and sprinkled ya with some of Trilata's energy she had magically extracted and mixed with her gold dust. Then she hummed *Life* which she'd written to make Trilata live through you – that tune was telling you, urging you not to die. And you didn't. To Trimoni, it was like her own baby not dying.'

I think my heart stopped because I couldn't hear it beat; I think my lungs were shocked into shutting too, as I couldn't feel my breath either.

I'd been infused with energy from a *magic* baby.

A *dying* baby. I went lumpy all over, and when my hands grabbed my head, my skull also felt bumpy. But my brain was pointing out that organs like hearts and kidneys from the dead often gave a new lease of life to the sick. Then what was so eerie about being granted, in my case, some energy to keep me alive?

'N-now I see how The Tune, er, *Life* got into my head,' I stuttered. 'And at last I know it was telling me to save Trilata by living. *Oh, my gosh!* My hunch about that tune saying something to me was correct. The funny thing was my mum felt Trimoni's gold dust was speaking to *her*.'

Alolla chuckled. 'That dust must have been emitting vibes of your wellbeing.'

Then sparked by a thought, I fired, 'But why couldn't Trimoni do magic to stop her own baby dying?'

'Magical communities like our Tree Folk have rules and laws about the use of magic. There are things we are not allowed to dabble with, such as the death of our folk. Death is sacred. We are not immortal and mature like Humans, although some do live for hundreds of years. If death does come early, it denotes *something*. There is the fear that saving Tree Folk from death by doing magic could leave them doomed or deformed.' Alolla held up her palm. 'The law says no to tampering with Tree-Folk deaths.'

Now I was balancing at the edge of my chair. 'Does this mean I've got m-magic in me?'

'Ya could have magic.' Alolla's voice softened. 'Trimoni's magic, Trilata's magic.'

'You can turn a toy to life, yes?'

Despite my failed organs, I managed a smile hearing Zylo shoot the same question I'd asked him when I first learned he was magical. 'I sometimes know things before they happen, like accidents,' I blurted. 'Then I rescue people, and everybody ends up thinking I'm weird. The kids at school make fun of me and –'

'Ah! Ya got Trimoni's protecting powers through Tri-lata. There could be more magic inside ya.'

'More magic! Really?'

'When Trimoni was a child, she first realised she had the special skill of protecting. Later, she showed healing powers also. So she trained in them at school.'

Zylo slid off his seat and did a handstand. 'There's a bit of *Tree Folk* in you!'

His words raged through my brain and made my head whirl, leaving me swaying on the chair.

Then what was I?

What was I?

Would it ever sink in that I was a little magical too?

'Get off the floor, boy, before ya injure yourself.' Alolla's voice sounded muffled amid the topsy-turvy in my mind.

'I haven't finished the story,' she added.

I heard her clearly.

Miss Fifi meowed as if she was eager to hear the rest of the tale. Zylo sprang onto a chair. I held my breath.

Chapter 14

'The family secret was safe for a while,' Alolla said. 'Trimoni and Rin had Zylo the next year. But about three years after that, Lord Grailib got to know what Trimoni had done.'

Miss Fifi yawned as though she was already bored.

'But Mama used magic to save a *Human* baby who was dying – so she didn't break the law!'

'Ah, creating a Pathway from our invisible woods to the Valley of Humans is also against the law. But Trimoni was more afraid to break the law of death, in case things went wrong and Trilata turned out doomed or deformed.'

'Then did a big bad thing happen to Mama for making a Pathway?' Zylo cried.

'Lord Grailib banished her from Bluebark Woods.'

'And she *died.*' Zylo beat his chest. 'She died!'

Alolla flung her hands out to Zylo, and he dashed to her side and fell on his knees. She arranged his hair into place with her fingers.

'Mama didn't die,' she said.

'Mama, Mama, Mama didn't die?' Zylo shot to his feet. 'Mama's not dead, Mama's not dead,' he repeated, plainly relishing hearing those words. 'Hate secrets, hate secrets!'

'Then where's Trimoni?' I butted in, holding hands with Zylo's tantrum.

Tears were bucketing down Alolla's face. 'She is living somewhere in the Valley of Humans.'

'Trimoni is living in one of our towns?'

Boy or not, now Zylo was crying as if he didn't know how to stop; he seemed to be unpacking the sobs he'd collected in his chest for years. He fell at Alolla's feet again. 'Why didn't you tell me Mama was in the valley?'

I rolled in Zylo's anguish.

'Oh, Zylo-boy, Papa and I were afraid to tell ya.'

'Why? *Why?* Couldn't be worse than thinking I don't have a mama, yes?'

'We were worried you'd go searching for her once ya grew up and had the power to create a Pathway from the woods to the valley. Ya might have been banished from the woods too for violating the law. We couldn't lose ya also. Papa would have died of grief. I haven't seen him make merry since Mama was taken away from him. Ya have to understand.'

'I wouldn't have wanted Papa to die of sad sickness.'

'But why is it a violation of the law to create a Pathway?' I asked.

Alolla rocked a little. 'We are not allowed to go to the Valley of Humans because our footsteps form a Pathway that Humans can use to get to our invisible woods – of course, only if they find that Pathway, like ya did.'

Only if? Only if? So that's what it was. I gasped, recalling how the arch in my wall never showed up when I slipped into my backyard from the kitchen, but became visible whenever I got into the yard through my bedroom window – which I now knew was along Trimoni's Pathway.

The vanishing arch was not a mystery anymore.

Oh, my gosh!

Alolla was studying my face silently, seemingly guessing my gasping meant I was distracted by my thoughts. Then seeing I was back with her, she said, 'If Humans arrive, they will chop down what is left of our trees. That will be the end of our kind in Bluebark

Valley.' Even sensible, practical Alolla shuddered. 'Creating a Pathway by crossing to the other side is the worst offence the Tree Folk can commit.'

Zylo's lips quivered. 'Th-then why did Mama do it?'

'Trimoni was in a terrible state of mind: she couldn't get past trying to keep Trilata alive. She wasn't thinking clearly ... Only Lord Grailib can go across to the Valley of Humans without giving rise to a Pathway.' Alolla's eyes became shifty. 'Makes me wonder whether he went there, when ages ago he disappeared often. Of course, he's been on magic-enhancement programs to other locations where Tree Folk live.' She tapped her chin. 'His trips away almost cost him his place as Lord because someone else took over. There was a commotion. Most of the Tree Folk backed Lord Grailib, and he was finally returned to his position, his birthright. Since then he has hardly left the woods, except to attend major magic-updating events.'

'Then can't I talk with Mama through the speak-o-port, Grammie?'

Alolla reached forward to Zylo, still on his knees, and cupped his chin with her palm. 'Papa and I tried that. We used all our magic to get through to her in the valley. Nothing worked. Of course we couldn't go there to find her because of the Pathways we'd form, increasing the chance of Human invasion.'

'Didn't Mama try to get to us?'

'She would have, she's a risk taker. And I have a dreaded feeling that something might have become of her. Even if she is safe, we don't know where she is. She escaped through the Pathway she created, before Lord Grailib could send her to a place of his choice. Yet she must be close to ya, Zylo-boy, close to the woods. With you living here, she wouldn't have left the valley.'

'Oh, then, with my bedroom being where her Pathway leads to, she could be in the town where I live.'

'She said ya were in a place called Crickle Town,' Alolla whispered. 'Is it near the woods?'

I shook my head up and down till it nearly fell off, and then gave Zylo a friendly shove. 'Wish you could go with me to Crickle Town to find her!'

'Can see no wall,' Zylo wailed.

'Oh, that's right,' I said, recalling our first encounter.

'There's a reason for that,' Alolla said. 'To begin with, a Tree-Folk child can't build a Wall of the Mind to cross over from our invisible woods to the Valley of Humans.'

'A Wall of the Mind?' I asked.

'The only way Tree-Folk adults can get to the Valley of Humans from these woods is through an arch they cut in a wall that they magically construct in their minds.

Being a creation of the *mind*, that wall with an arch can be seen by only the Tree-Folk person who built it. That's why other Tree Folk, including Zylo, can't spot Trimoni's wall.'

'Oh, my gosh, is the endless wall I clap eyes on when crossing back to the valley from the woods, Trimoni's Wall of the Mind?'

'Ah!' Alolla nodded. 'The reason you're able to see it is this: because the woods were made invisible to keep the Tree Folk and Humans apart, if a Tree-Folk person goes to the Valley of Humans, it triggers, in magical terms, an invitation for Humans to also visit the invisible woods. That's why a Pathway to allow Humans into the woods is formed by a Tree-Folk person's footsteps – well, except the Lord's footsteps because Grailib magic recognises that no invitation is intended.'

Alolla paused, as if to give me time to digest what she was saying. 'So, Humans travelling on a *Pathway* along the invisible woods will see a Wall of the Mind with an arch, so that they are able to cross back to the valley – just as they'll see that arch to be able to enter the invisible woods, if they are on that Pathway along the valley. But on the valley side, the arch gets embedded into a *real* wall at the point where the Tree-Folk person slipped into the Valley of Humans.'

'Trimoni's arch is in my backyard wall which borders the woods,' I cried. 'Never imagined that a simple stone wall could be harbouring magic.'

'Oh, so it's through your backyard that Trimoni made her way to ya. We never knew, because she remained silent about where her Pathway was, given that other Tree Folk couldn't even see her Wall of the Mind.'

The blood rushed to my face. 'Ooh, now that I know that that long wall I see is what Trimoni built on the wood side, I get why I lose sight of it once I return to my backyard. And, Zylo, we at last have the explanation for your not seeing a wall with an arch when I did.'

'We can also understand why you didn't believe I was doing cartwheels in the grass,' Zylo said. 'All *you* could see was Mama's wall.'

'Astounding!' I said. 'Now I must go find Trimoni.'

Zylo put up his toothiest grin.

Miss Fifi's eyes seemed to bulge.

'Will help if you give me the clearest photo you've got of her,' I said.

'Photo?' Alolla asked.

'Picture of her.'

'Afraid, my old hands are not very good at sketching –'

'I mean a camera shot.'

Alolla and Zylo exchanged puzzled glances.

I realised then that photography too hadn't clicked its way into the lives of the Tree Folk.

'Wait,' Alolla said, rising from her chair. She went up-stairs, and returned, dipping her fingers into a weeny wooden box. Zylo and I crowded around her. From under a piece of white lace, she plucked a disk pendant. On the face of it was an intricately designed T. She held it up by its equally delicate chain. 'This was made for baby Trilata, just like the pendant Trimoni always wore. Take it with ya. If Trimoni has got her one on, ya will recognise her because there won't be another T like this on your side. Engraving of this type is the traditional work of the Tree Folk.'

'What if she is not wearing the pendant?' I asked.

'Still, if ya find her, this could be your way of proving to her that ya have met me. And it's hard to miss that long golden mane, which flowed like a shimmering river.'

'That was a long time ago,' I said gently. 'She may have cut her hair or changed its colour.'

'My Trimoni is tall and slender,' Alolla kept going, 'and has a long face like Zylo's.'

Zylo put on a funny look and succeeded in making his real face appear longer.

Alolla sighed, and I got the feeling that beneath her optimism were the same doubts I had.

'Unless Trimoni is wearing her pendant, tracking her won't be easy,' I said. 'You Tree Folk look so much like us.'

'Watch out for *beaky* ears,' Zylo cut in.

'True, her ears won't go unnoticed in Crickle Town, but that is the very reason she's bound to hide them. Tell you what I'll do,' I said. 'I'll search for a lady who never takes off her headgear!'

Chapter 15

I was eager to get to school the next morning. It wasn't because I thought Sky was going to add me to her gang or even acknowledge my existence at Crickle Town Primary. It was because, where better to start my search than at school given that Trimoni had been a teacher on the other side? She may have got a similar job on this.

I slipped Trimoni's pendant into my pocket, hoping for a day of findings. When I got to school, I emulated a health-and-safety inspector and walked briskly around the corridors and grounds.

No Trimoni-possibles.

Then, during our English class, I put on an I-am-about-to-burst face and excused myself to go to the toilet. This allowed me to peek into other classes in progress for a teacher in headgear.

None.

At recess, I ducked my head around the staff room door as if I wanted a word with Ms Upton. Luckily, she wasn't there. And teachers who were there weren't hiding their ears. I paid a visit to other parts of the school like the staff office, administration office and educational support room.

No again.

When we got to the last period for the day which was drama class, I was as excited as the others but for a different reason. Could Trimoni who had been a drama teacher at Bluebark Tree School, have slipped into the same post here?

By the time we got to the school hall, I could barely hear myself think. The buzz was about the Year 6 play, and I recalled Sky saying it was this term's biggie. Probably seeing I was standing around solo, Ava, the Assertive, waltzed up to me with a smile. It didn't look as if she'd ripped off my *hero* label and replaced it with a *freak* label – well, not as yet.

'The first class for the term is always exciting,' she said, 'because Miss Dawson tells us what play we are going to do.'

Ava was hushed by the drama teacher's arrival, but

my mind couldn't be silenced from squealing, *Trimoni slim, Trimoni tall* ...

And oh, my gosh, her ears were covered also.

She had on a sequin-on-silk beanie.

I stood gulping like a goldfish, rummaging for my voice. 'Does Miss Dawson always wear a beanie?'

'Nice colour,' Ava responded.

'Yeah, but does she –'

'Good to see you all looking fresh and sprightly after the holidays,' Miss Dawson said, putting down the stack of paper in her hands. 'We have exciting stuff to keep us on our toes this term.'

'What's the Year 6 play going to be, Miss?' Bea was almost tipping over her.

'Patience is a virtue, Bea.' Miss Dawson made two piles of the paper on the table and adjusted her beanie.

She's making certain her ears are not showing, I told myself.

'This term we are going to perform *The Little Mermaid* by Hans Christian Anderson,' Miss Dawson said.

Enthused sounds whizzed round the hall with lots of hands hitting the air. Sky and her gang were moving their arms in the same manner. Had they practised a cheer routine to usher in the announcement?

Miss Dawson seemed rapt at the response. 'I am sure

most of you know the story, but for those of you who don't, I have included a summary in there,' she said, pointing at the piles on the table. 'In a nutshell, it's about a mermaid princess from an underwater kingdom saving a human prince from a shipwreck – and then wanting to become a human being in order to be with him.'

She toyed with her beanie again, and my heart fluttered.

'To give us more time to practise, I'm going to start off the term by giving you some passages from the major roles.' Miss Dawson pointed at the green sheets. 'And lines from the minor roles.' She pointed at the white sheets. 'You can decide what role you want to try out for and grab the relevant paper. I'll give you time today to read through the parts, and next week I want you to come with the one you're interested in well memorised. I'll be doing the casting.'

Miss Dawson was rewarded again with plenty of oohing and wowing.

She smiled at the boys. 'Any takers for sailors?'

The sounds the boys made could have meant great or gross. I tell you, sometimes I wonder whether boys are a different species. Of course, Mum says my thinking will change soon.

While waiting till the scramble for the scripts was

over, I observed Miss Dawson, wishing I had more than two eyes, two ears, one nose, one mind and one brain with which to suss her. Then I helped myself to a white paper and ran my eyes through the roles.

'What part are you going for?' Vera asked, peeping at what I was reading.

'Not sure,' I said. 'Hey, isn't Miss Dawson's beanie ace? Does she wear those all the time?'

Vera grinned. 'Been here for several terms and never seen her without a headdress.'

My stomach did something like Zylo's somersaults. Okay, so, how was I going to check whether the ears beneath that beanie were *beaky*? I kept watching Miss Dawson weaving her tall self around the students, discussing the roles and answering their questions. I had only one query:

Was Miss Dawson of Crickle Town really Trimoni of Bluebark Woods?

When the class ended, the others scurried out of the hall, while I had to drag myself. Then all in a moment, I was at the table where Miss Dawson was collecting the remaining sheets of paper. Before I realised what I was doing, I had plucked off her beanie.

What I saw was a bald head with ears no longer than mine.

I gasped at my own audacity while Miss Dawson covered her head with her hands. Her face was crimson.

'I'm sorry,' I cried, handing back her beanie. 'I'm new in town and was looking to buy some headgear and, and I've never seen such a cool beanie ...' I wolfed down a breath. 'I should have asked first.' My chest tightened, wondering whether what she was wearing was a chemo cap.

Miss Dawson put on the beanie, her face still reddish. Then, she wallowed in laughter. 'I like a girl with spunk,' she said, 'going after what she wants. But the next person you try that on may not be as forgiving.'

When I left the hall, Sky was hovering around the door. 'Did you think Miss Dawson's beanie had got stuck to her head?' she asked, arching her brow. Then she turned her back on me and marched off – reducing me to jelly.

Was Sky now spying on me?

An after-school snoop too didn't pay dividends, so instead of going home, I headed to the high street. Plan B was to check whether Trimoni, being a musician and a music teacher, had taken a job in the local music store I had noticed the other day.

Standing outside the store, I gathered my wits together while reading the sign above the door: 'Music Box'. How quaint. I entered what instantly felt a cosy nest – the type of place in which a person in disguise might take refuge. Then I headed along the aisle formed by shelves of music books to the left, and the long tables of CDs I'd spotted through the windows the other day to the right. When I got to the counter, the sales assistant was slipping a few CDs into a bag for a customer. The assistant had honey-coloured hair floating past her waist and around her head she was wearing a cloth that looked like a yoga band.

The band concealed the upper half of her ears.

My heart swelled with hope even as my stomach rumbled at what I'd done to Miss Dawson. Soon the other customer was walking away and the assistant was tilting her head at me, but my mind was busy judging that her face was long enough to be grouped with Zylo's.

'What are you after?' she asked.

My eyes dropped to her bare neck and sent my hands into my pocket. Then I looked up at her and found that she was now bending over the counter.

'Yesterday, I lost a pendant just like this one,' I said, opening the wooden box and popping it by her. 'I'm going back to the places I visited in case I'd left it behind and someone put it away.'

The assistant picked up the pendant and turned it about on her palm. 'What a treasure! I've never seen such workmanship. Is it from overseas?'

I squeezed out all my hopes, and the strain must have shown on my face.

'Oh, look at me rabbiting on,' she said. 'I was here yesterday. Nobody handed in any lost property.' She placed the pendant in its box. 'Is this one your mum's? Your grandma's?'

'Gran's.'

'Must be how jewellery was crafted in those days. Not like some of the crap we see nowadays. You must be feeling mad at losing yours.'

'Well, at least Gran's pendant is safe,' I said, tucking it back into my pocket and trying to pack away my disappointment too.

'Sorry I don't have good news for you.'

'No worries,' I said, and shuffled out of the shop, pumping my brain for Plan C.

Chapter 16

Home before Mum, I sat in the kitchen having my tea, and it must have gone straight to my head because in a shot I had Plan C.

I'd make flyers offering my weekend services for odd jobs in homes. I reckoned I'd pass off as older than my age because of my height, so I could go from door to door rather than putting the flyers into people's mail boxes. True, I'd get a mouthful from some for dragging them to the door for a flyer, but at least this wasn't the city where people measured their time in money. Besides, I was willing to take the flak in return for a chance to peep at people in their houses as they were unlikely to be wearing headgear indoors – even a pointy-eared Trimoni might have let her guard down at home.

I was soon spread at the kitchen table drafting a flyer. But I kept ripping my efforts, fearing they didn't sound legit. Just then Mum trudged in with a pile of books and landed them on the table.

'What's all this for?' I asked.

'How about, "How are you, Mum? How has your day been?"' She allowed herself a noisy yawn. 'I've had an exhausting day. And I've brought home more work – to do some additional research for my report.'

'On the Highway?'

'Mmm, I must say the staff at Crickle Town Library were very helpful.'

'Passed the place on Sunday when I went for a walk,' I said absently.

Library staff … As if it had waited for prompting, my brain released a stored snippet: Trimoni's library style. Oh, yeah, Zylo also said that Rin had pronounced her a librarian. With those traits, could she have learned the required skills to land a job at the local library?

I made an entry in my mental diary to visit the library tomorrow.

When I got to school the next morning, the place was agog. Then it struck me that the school photos were going to be taken. Plenty of students and teachers were already assembling under the gum tree near the principal's office.

I decided to dump my schoolbag in class before joining the others. As I scurried along the main passage, I felt my temperature rising – I was baking like a muffin. My heart, I think, was bursting. And taking over from my eyes that were going misty was again a light in my mind. It was showing me that gum tree where the others were gathering. I was sure now it was the first signs of a disaster relating to the tree. Rubbing my eyes, I twisted my head. More scuttling to the spot. I had to do something.

Oh, my gosh, I was about to make a witch of myself in front of the *whole* school.

I swallowed, recalling the battering I'd got from the anguish and guilt of nearly not rescuing Ava. I'd hated myself every second, and counting. It was how *I* felt about myself that mattered, not what others thought.

I had to believe in myself.

But how was I going to get everyone quickly away from the tree?

My yelling construed as a prank had got a group stuck in a lift in Moon City. I dived into my brain for an alternative and found my feet suddenly hammering towards the school hall.

I reached for the fire alarm in the hallway and pulled down the trigger.

The school was clanging with the sound of the fire bell.

The next was to get to the tree to assess the aftermath of my action. I plunged forward but crashed into another girl who was racing from the building.

My victim was Bea.

'W-where's the fire?' she asked, between gasping and trying to remain on her feet.

I opened my mouth, yet delivered nothing.

'Come on, playground, the place to go in case of fire.' Bea was poking her head in every direction. 'Where? Where?'

I stared at her blankly.

Bea rolled her eyes to the right and then to the left. 'There is no fire, is there? Another one of your peculiar –'

I dashed past Bea, leaving her to complete her sentence; what I didn't hear couldn't hurt. And, whoa, everyone was scarpering to the playground. No-one was under the tree. Not even the cameraman.

My gambit had worked.

Just as Bea caught up with me, a large branch of that gum tree, under which most of the school had been standing, came crashing down. The branch lay there like a strapping dead body, occupying a good part of the ground.

Terrified shrieks followed.

Then Bea flung her arms above her head and waved them from side-to-side shouting, 'No fire! No fire!'

A sudden quiet fell over the hysteria.

Mrs Barker, the principal, and Ms Upton were marching towards us.

'Marvel pulled the alarm handle as a joke,' Bea said when they arrived.

I hunted for my voice, but another beat me to it.

'That branch falling was no better than a fire,' the voice said. 'We were all by that tree minutes ago.'

Sky was standing right next to me, panting, red-faced and dishevelled.

I stood a hero.

By now others were crowding around us, and hosting the party was Bea. It didn't take Einstein to figure that I-love-to-stir Bea was stuffing their heads with what had happened in class and at the park. I could sense my heroism dissipating as necks were twisted to take a peek at me.

Way more faces than at class were wearing the witch-or-fairy? look.

I froze on the outside and burnt inside.

'We have had a narrow shave, and we are all shaken,' Mrs Barker said. 'Sky is right – there does appear to be a silver lining in *this* lark.' She glanced at me. 'We will deal with this matter in my office. I will see you at recess.' Then she surveyed the area housing the massive branch as if she was considering declaring it a disaster zone. 'The photographs will be rescheduled for another day.'

I turned to thank Sky – yeah, Sky – who only yesterday had given me the wobbles. But she was making her way back to her gang. Nobody had ever stood up for me at school. Nobody.

I blinked back the tears and tried to call out to her, but a lump in my throat got in the way.

Chapter 17

I got away with a week's after-school detention and a warning from Mrs Barker and Ms Upton who was also present at the principal's office at recess. They said I'd committed a *hideous crime* (my slightly exaggerated version), but that they were letting me off lightly only this once as I was new in school and in town – all of which had to mean some adjustment blah, blah, blah. Little did they know I'd bidden a happy farewell to my life in the city. Wouldn't worry Mum with what I'd done, they added. Again, just this time. The other thing they mentioned was that given the way things had panned out, the school owed me some gratitude. They got that last one right.

I got the feeling their solemn eyes would be spying on me 24/7 which was daunting enough. But, I tell you, what made me emit nervous energy till I went limp was the witch-or-fairy? looks that, thanks to Bea, were making a comeback.

I carried my limp self out of the school an hour later than the others because of my detention. Yet, surprisingly, I detected a glow in my heart. I had dropped my worry about what it would do to me – big time – and plugged into action.

That action had saved a *whole* school.

I was warmed by the privilege – yeah, privilege – of being able to do what I did. Maybe I was the lucky one. I couldn't help seeing myself in a new light.

And that allowed me to focus on putting a smile on the face of my only friend.

I hit the high street.

I entered the Crickle Town Library and pushed past the swivelling barrier, my eyes on the book handling counter.

The hatless woman helping readers check out books had ears nothing short of human. I took myself to the centre of the library where there was a triangular information counter. Two women and a man lost behind computers were assisting readers. They were not the person I was searching for.

I wedged my way around the aisles looking for other

staff stacking shelves with returned books and so on, and soon reached the back of the library. Seeing a half-opened door, I peeked into what was labelled the *Meeting Room,* to find a long table with chairs and a huge white board. No ears. The next room was marked the *Resources Room.* Through the glass panels, I could see a few people again at computers and a human helper hovering over them. I groaned. I was getting nowhere.

Trimoni, Trimoni, where are you?

Just then I saw a trolley full of books parked by some rotating bookstands. Oh, at last. I hastened towards the cart, expecting to bump into a staff member attending to the load. Before I got there, a woman suddenly appeared at the top of a staircase I hadn't noticed.

'What's in the basement?' I whispered, pointing my thumbs down while sadly noting her utterly human ears.

'More books and Kiddies' Corner.' The woman tapped her smiling lips with her finger. 'Story time in progress.'

I made my way down the narrow staircase and then around the lines of shelves. No luck. Still, all was not lost. I could revert to my door-to-door flyer delivery scheme, couldn't I? Then, from the maze of books, I emerged at the front left side of the library and landed in Kiddies' Corner. Children were sitting cross-legged on the floor clustered around a low chair.

The lady on it was reading a book in an animated tone. She was wearing a buttercup yellow, sleeveless dress which skirted the floor around her feet. Her hair was tucked into a pre-prepared floral scarf that had a large side-bow.

That scarf was also covering her ears.

My stomach outdid Zylo's cartwheels. I could have kicked myself for getting unduly hopeful as at school and the music store. Was I heading for another blow? True, she was slender. True, she appeared all limbs like me and possibly taller than average when she stood. So what? There were heaps of slim, tall women, as Miss Dawson had proved. Heaps of scarf-wearing women. Oh, Zylo, Zylo, I wish there was more to go by.

Then I recalled there was, and my gaze shifted to the storyteller's neck. She *was* wearing a pendant, and it was round like Trilata's disk. My heart flipped. I closed up to the group, yet my eyes couldn't make the distance to grab the detail.

Seeing I'd have to wait, I slid behind the shelves nearby to prevent anyone wondering why a hulking girl was indulging in story time. No sooner had I hidden, than I was scowling at the sound of a low voice from the adjoining aisle. Next it was a muffled laugh. Oh, what? I peeped around the corner to confirm my suspicion.

Sky was with her gang, raiding the shelves.

Country town syndrome. I crunched my teeth. How was I going to approach the storyteller with them hanging around? Hadn't I already made a spectacle of myself at school? Any slip now would reach Crickle Town Primary on the count of one. I backed away with the eyes of Mrs Barker and Ms Upton playing havoc in my mind. Luckily, Sky and the others hadn't spotted me. Not as yet.

I had to play hide-and-seek with them while notching to high alert for the end of story time. The double act exhausted me. Finally, the gang was moving away. I kept my distance but stole after them until I saw their feet disappear up the steps. Done.

Then I ducked back to Kiddies' Corner to the sound of children's voices and the shuffling of feet. The storyteller was peeking into her handbag. She was standing; she was tall. In a daze, I dipped into my pocket and fished out the jewellery box.

With a plan of its own, my hand reached for Trilata's disk and clasped the chain around my neck.

I edged up to the storyteller's elbow. 'Miss,' I said softly, not wanting to startle her.

Her eyes shifted to me. Mine shifted to her round pendant.

I blinked hard, to see it a second time.

Her pendant wasn't engraved with a T.

'Yes?' she asked, offering me an uncertain smile.

'Oh, sorry,' I managed, turning into a lump of despair. 'I thought you were someone else.'

I got no response because her gaze had dropped from my face to the disk I was wearing.

Her eyes were ogling the disk.

Then she jerked her head back and glanced every way, before pointing at my neck with a long, trembling finger. 'Where did you get that p-pendant?'

'My grandmother –'

'*No! Not a Human's!* I, I mean ...' Her face was chalky; her chest was heaving.

My heart thudded. 'You mean – the pendant belongs to the Tree Folk of Bluebark Woods?'

Chapter 18

'You're not a Tree-Folk girl!' The storyteller sounded as if she was accusing me for not being one.

'But I know Zylo.'

She placed her palm on her heart. '*My* Zylo? My little boy?'

'Trimoni's Zylo.'

Her eyes almost fell out. 'How do you know us? You've been to the woods?'

Despite the wisps of doubt surfacing in my mind with her not wearing the T pendant, I said, 'I got to the woods by following your path from my bedroom.'

'From your bedroom?' Her eyes were now oozing with feathery softness. She touched my arm ever so gently – I felt like a china doll. 'You were the Human baby who was dying.'

Would she know that if she wasn't Trimoni?

'Alolla told me you saved my life,' I said, dropping more crumbs to check her out.

Her hands instantly went to her cheeks because the softness in her eyes had transformed into tears. 'My baby Trilata lives on in you.'

My heart clapped, but still came the urge to yank off her scarf. Fearing I might, I tucked my hands away in my pockets and asked, 'Why aren't you wearing your T pendant?'

'Oh, my T?' She dived into her handbag and came up with a pouch. 'I didn't want to rouse suspicion by wearing something never seen here before.' Then with a catch in her throat she added, 'I couldn't risk the safety of the woods, done enough damage as it is. Carrying the T around was the only way to stay close to my family.' She unzipped the tiny case.

And out of it came a disk pendant engraved with a T.

It was identical to the pendant around my neck.

I got home intending to fly out of my window and tell Zylo I had found his mama.

Mum had other ideas.

Already back from work, she was cooking for an old

friend from the valley she had invited to dinner. She wanted my help though all I could add to a pot was finger juice. Her other request was that I hung around to be introduced to her friend. I didn't think I'd be dinner party material with the conversation I'd had with Trimoni, after seeing her pendant, playing in my head like an endless CD. But Mum rarely asked me for a favour.

So I had to wait till after school the next day.

I couldn't wait to see Zylo's reaction to my news: would he stand on his hands, do a backflip, a somersault or what? Savouring the moment, I peeked through the opened window of his living room. Alolla was sitting motionless, seemingly forgetting the chair could rock. Miss Fifi was on the floor between Alolla's feet, demoted from her lap. Rin slumped on a chair opposite them with his head buried in his hands. Zylo wasn't even there.

Their body language told me something was amiss.

Were they just having a down day? Or anxious about my finding Trimoni? My heart smiled. Wait, I said to myself, till I change all that. I dashed round the tree and in my excitement banged on the door.

Alolla's tearstained face and the air hugging the room got me feeling I had entered a graveyard. 'Is everything okay?'

Rin dragged his head away from his palms as if he was peeping out of a torture chamber. His wettish hair was combed back, as it had been at the market square, and he had a sad slant to his mouth.

Dismissing my question, Alolla shuffled up to Rin. 'Zylo's papa.'

'Hello, there,' I said, cautiously bright. 'I'm Marvel.'

'It's Zylo,' he said, clearly needing no introduction and unsurprised to see me. 'It's Zylo.'

'Zylo?' I glanced at the stairs expecting him to bounce down the steps.

'They've taken him,' Alolla whimpered. 'They've taken him.'

I stared from one to the other. 'Taken him? Who? Where?'

'Lord Grailib came to know that Zylo was getting help to search for his mama,' Alolla said.

'*What?*'

Miss Fifi stretched, appearing listless despite the events that had taken place.

Alolla fell back into her chair. 'He has sent Zylo to the dungeons.'

'No! No! I've found Trimoni –'

'*You found Trimoni?*' Rin shot off his chair, nearly knocking his head on the wooden ceiling.

'She's working at our local library,' I said, seating my-self.

'Was she – that woman – wearing the pendant?' Again, Alolla's straight-to-the-point tone complemented her centre parting.

'It was in her handbag. Yeah, the genuine article.' I got Trilata's box from my pocket and handed it back to Alolla.

She held it to her heart the way one would her last possession. Tears were pelting down her cheeks. 'How is Trimoni? What did she tell ya? Why didn't she get in touch with us?'

'She's lovely,' I said, my eyes flitting between Alolla and Rin. 'Given what happened to her, she is in good spirits too.'

'That's my Trimoni,' Rin said.

'She told me Lord Grailib had cut her off all magical lines of communication with the woods.'

Alolla wagged her finger. 'That's what I thought! Shows why we couldn't get to her through the speak-o-port.'

'Trimoni also said that Lord Grailib had promised to put Zylo away if she sneaked back to visit him.'

'And that's exactly what he has done – put Zylo away!' Alolla said.

'The scoundrel!' Rin began pacing the floor. 'How dare he threaten my beloved?'

I frowned. 'Why isn't my mind showing me the danger Zylo is in as it does with others?'

'You're probably limited to the people around ya.'

'That won't stop me,' I said. 'I'll go to the Lord and beg him for Zylo's release.'

Alolla's eyes lit with fear. 'He'll pounce on ya, capture ya, turn ya to meat. Lord Grailib must be angst you'll show other Humans Trimoni's Pathway.'

Rin flopped into a chair, rubbing his chin. 'Going to him is no good. You'll also be sent to those unforgiving dungeons below his mansion.'

'Zylo must be petrified,' I said.

Rin hid his head in his palms again. Was he trying to escape from images of Zylo in prison? My eyes rested on Alolla. She was polishing her face with a lace handkerchief – maybe she was hoping that would wipe off her pain.

I sprang off the chair. 'I must go!' I said, pumping my voice with more *oomph* than I felt.

Rin lifted his head and glanced at Alolla. I had the strangest feeling they were conversing with no words. Miss Fifi was twisting her neck and watching them as though she was in on what was being said.

I wasn't, but my worried ears listened to the silence.

Then Alolla picked up the notebook on the table next to her, and blew at a page. A map appeared.

I blinked.

'See for yourself how complicated it is. Ya don't even know the woods. Don't go to the mansion!'

I stared at the web of streets and swallowed.

'We've already tried to persuade Lord Grailib to return Zylo to us,' Rin said. 'But our pleas didn't move even a muscle on his face. It's no use.'

'It's my fault you have lost Zylo also.'

'Ya have found Trimoni. You're Zylo's true friend. You're brave, but ...' Alolla crumpled the map and let it drop to the ground. 'W-we can't let ya come to harm. You're the closest we have to Trilata ... Trilata ...'

'You have some of my daughter in you,' Rin said in a voice that couldn't belong to a person who had supposedly stored away his emotions. His eyes were pleading.

Something about them took me to a deep place. A place where misfortune and ill-treatment couldn't win over love. These folk had enough love to share with even me. I had to put Zylo back in their fold. For a moment, I watched Alolla, now buried in sobs with her eyes shut, and then Rin who'd sunk back into his palms. I reached for the map on the floor and tiptoed to the door.

Oh, no, I didn't know the door magic.

I turned back in time to watch Miss Fifi stealing out of the window. She was little; she could do it. Would I get squashed? *Why* didn't I try that magic when Zylo told me the window was possible to climb out of though small from the outside? Well, at least I was skinny. I slunk to the window and lifted myself to it. Then I held my stomach in and shut my eyes ...

When I opened them, I was standing, unscarred, by a flowerbed.

I let out a sigh. Then I glared at the map, without the foggiest idea as to how I was going to win over the Lord of Bluebark Woods.

Lord Grailib.

Chapter 19

I paused at the top of Seedturf Street, squinting at the signboard. Which way should I turn? According to Alolla's map, Rootberry Street was to the right, but the road sign pointed left. Poor Alolla. Her despair had to have taken a toll on her brain, er, her breath more like it. I followed the sign and trudged along the street until I got to the next junction where her map required me to go left. The problem was the same. The board signalled right. Once more, I went with the sign and continued to do so as the discrepancy occurred again and again.

Now I was on Stemstone Street and my skin was becoming crawly. What was happening to the trees? The trunks? Where were the doors and windows? Were the Tree Folk being invaded again in some way?

Creatures!

Forming on the trunks were tree monsters. Why were they nodding their huge, long heads as if disapproving my trip? I yelped seeing spirits, tree spirits, emerge like skeletons. Even their vacant looks seemed to be mocking me. Did they reckon I'd never make it to the Lord's? I could hear a bump, bump, bump; I think it was my heart. Eyeing me from trees on both sides of the street were demons. They were grinning wickedly, displaying sharp, red teeth which made me shudder. Then I was at the mercy of tree dragons with enormous wings. Oh, no, they were positioning themselves to scoop me up. But would the tree nymphs get me first? Their eyes were squirting fire in my direction. I was sweating, I was huffing, I was puffing – would I burst into flames? Why were they also against me?

Was this what Alolla's cautionary warning had meant? Complicated or not, I couldn't turn back; I had to reunite Zylo with his mama. How was a kid supposed to cope without a mother? 'Mum, Mum,' I called, to stop myself from going gaga. Then the fear of reducing to ashes and never seeing her dwarfed my terror of the creatures. I jacked up my speed.

Soon I was forced to slow down because the roots of the trees were surfacing and wriggling like snakes. They were spreading all over and narrowing the street. Some roots were as thick as branches, and I had to hop over them to get by. Again, I got the feeling I was being stopped.

Then I landed on a rocky bridge that wasn't marked on Alolla's map. Was I going the wrong way? Ouch. Stones were piercing my feet through the soles of my shoes. And when I peeked at the stream below the bridge, shark-like creatures were raising their faces to me. I trembled, picturing the bridge collapsing and myself tumbling into their open jaws.

Finally, I got to the other side. Baybranch Street. Like the bridge, it wasn't on Alolla's map. Did Alolla's breath forget to insert them? Or was I lost in the woods? Terror catapulted from my mouth.

Then quiet came.

The woods were back to what they were; the trunks were houses.

Heaving several breaths, I flung my arms out to embrace the woods. How did that happen? With my head still reeling, I got no answers but, I tell you, I'd escaped *Hell Street*.

When I got to the end of Baybranch Street, I was in a cul-de-sac. My eyes darted from tree to tree, gleaning for help until my gaze settled on one tree house. Unlike the others, it extended beyond the trunk into a sort of wooden house on stilts. A staircase led to a landing which had a door to the extension. Hanging on that door there was a board with bright lettering:

Conielle's Cakes & Sweets.

Conielle? Zylo's family friend? Her sweetshop? If her, I could get proper instructions to Leaflog Street where, according to the map, Lord Grailib lived. Sensing a safety net, even my toenails turned warm. I sailed up the steps and knocked on the door. After a while I gave it another try. Still hearing nothing, I shifted along the landing and peeped through the window.

The shop shelves were crammed with gleaming glass jars filled with sweets in a myriad of colours. The sweets dazzled my eyes. Were they dipped in magic? I tapped on the window, my mouth now watering at the sight of the treats on the long dresser in the middle of the shop. The assortment of cakes and jellies, which had toppings that appeared richer and creamier than anything I'd eaten, had to have a touch of magic too. I was licking my lips when a woman entered the shop and spotted me.

She had horns – *yeah, hair-horns!* And in a trifle, she was at the door, consuming me with her eyes in Conielle-fashion. 'Zylo's pal!' She began clicking her fingers.

'Bepa,' I said, gulping down my real name.

'Bepa it is.' Conielle treated me to her hyena cackle. 'A bag of sweets?'

'Er, I've lost my way, actually. I am trying to visit a friend down Leaflog Street.'

'Oh, easy.' Conielle smiled. 'Easier – why don't I walk you to Flowerdon Street where I'm setting off to? It's a road away from Leaflog Street.'

'Would you? Thanks!' I wanted to crash around like an overexcited five-year-old.

'Come in while I collect a few things,' she said.

Mentally clapping my hands, I went into Conielle's tree house. Now I was standing in a hallway where the trunk of the tree entered the wooden house through the roof. I got no more than a glimpse of a tree-shaped hat stand, ripe with hats and shawls, before Conielle tapped my shoulder. Then around the trunk to the back of the house and into a tiny room I was following her – but not on my feet.

I was floating just above the ground.

And Conielle was throwing her arms around like the conductor of an orchestra while mumbling something.

Then I found myself lying on a bed with my body wrapped in rope. My wrists were tied together, and my chest, waist and ankles were strapped to the bed. I couldn't budge. 'Let me off!' I squealed, trying to struggle and wincing as the rope cut into my flesh. 'Have you gone bats?'

'You won't be visiting Lord Grailib right now,' Conielle said.

'*Lord Grailib?* What are you on about?'

'Don't play games with me *Bepa,* you meddling Human girl.'

Human?

Human?

My quivering body sat in a dungeon while my mind ducked to avoid arrows.

'I know you've hunted down Trimoni,' Conielle ranted on. 'You're trying to get Trimoni back with Zylo and Rin. Trimoni should stay away, as ordered, considering what she did.'

My heart and pulse were racing each other. 'How do you know what Trimoni *did*?'

Conielle gave me another dose of her hyena treatment. 'By listening to that family nattering about it of course.'

'They would never have! Not in the presence of anyone.'

'I am not *anyone*,' Conielle said. 'I'm their mewing pet.'

Chapter 20

Conielle's eyes turned yellow.

I screeched.

Then whiskers grew to the left of her mouth.

I screamed.

And then to the right.

I shrieked.

Now a black bushy tail was wagging behind her.

I went dead silent.

Conielle was moving in ripples and dark rings of air were forming around her body. Through those rings a black cat emerged.

Conielle was gone.

Instead, sitting at the foot of the bed I was lying on, was Miss Fifi.

My heart pounded. 'You, you are *Conielle*?'

'Mew.' The cat was seemingly owning up.

'Noooo!' I cried, sick in my stomach. 'Get me off this bed, whoever you are! Get me off this bed!'

Miss Fifi morphed back into a Tree-Folk woman.

I blinked, hoping my eyes were tricking me, but standing over me was none other than Conielle. 'I c-can't understand,' I stuttered. 'Alolla, Rin and Zylo are also magic folk. How come they didn't realise *you* were their pet cat?'

'Did a great job, didn't I?' Conielle looked smug. 'I morph better than most in the woods. Made sure I left no tale-tell signs. Changing form is my special skill.'

I gasped, recalling Alolla also mention special skills. 'But why would you want to stop Zylo and Rin seeing Trimoni?'

'Listen here, you tiresome Human girl. The day Trimoni and Rin married, I swore I'd find a way to get Rin back.'

I whistled silently; Zylo, you were right about Conielle.

'He was my girlhood crush, my secret love,' she kept on. 'When they lost their first baby, I thought that might pull them apart. But no. They went on to have Zylo. I decided that doing nothing wasn't the way to get what I want. I became their pet to stay informed of what went on in their lives. That way I could strike when the opportunity arrived.'

Things like this never happen, my mind squeaked, but my head was throbbing with the links it was making: Alolla saying Miss Fifi often went missing; Miss Fifi's presence whenever the family was talking even to me. And, yeah, the way that cat looked bored and uninterested during some of the revelations and crises because they, as I now gathered, were *old* news to her. 'You're gross, twisted, barmy!' I burst out.

My insults had clearly missed their target because Conielle carried on. 'Then I got my chance one day when I heard Trimoni chatting with Alolla and Rin – Trimoni referred to her escapade to a spot called Crickle Town in the Valley of Humans to make certain her daughter lived on in some form.'

'So, it was *you* who told Lord Grailib Trimoni's secret.'

'Aren't you clever, Bepa, or *Trilata*, should I say!' Conielle smirked. 'And his decision to rid the woods of Trimoni – now wasn't that sweet? Lord Grailib rewarded me generously for reporting on an issue that could put the woods in peril, and for keeping my lips sealed about the whole matter to avoid panic. Oh, yes, I was made a member of the most esteemed magic group in the woods: the Lord's Circle.'

My head was now vibrating again, making more connections. 'Miss Fifi, I mean *you,* were at Zylo's when I asked Alolla about the harp music and showed her the gold dust –'

'Ha! Juicy stuff. Quenched my thirst.'

'And got you dashing to Lord Grailib again – this time to tell him I was to search for Trimoni.'

'Spot on!' Conielle flung her head back, and my ears had to listen to her laugh. 'Sending that brat to the dungeons – another of Lord Grailib's syrupy punishments.'

'Rin is still pinning for Trimoni,' I warned. 'The longer Trimoni is away, the more he will want her.'

'Rot! I'll get Rin in the end.'

'You can't buy him with sweets,' I retorted, reflecting on the heart-shaped box of goodies Conielle had urged Zylo to give Rin.

'The best way to a man's heart is through his belly, my ma used to tell me.'

I wanted to pull ugly faces and hurl names at her because being tied allowed me to do little else, but I got distracted by something fishy. 'Oh, my gosh, Miss Fifi, er, you were at Zylo's earlier this afternoon when I left for the Lord's mansion. You didn't want me to go there, *did* you?'

Conielle's smile was impish. 'Messed a teensy-weensy

bit with the road signs. But thank me for fluffing up a few friendly faces so that you didn't feel lonely –'

'The monsters, demons, dragons!' I croaked. 'They weren't real? Just you trying to scare me off?'

'Well, brave Human girl, the final victory was mine, because I made certain that if you couldn't be stopped from your jaunt, you'd be lured to my house. You *won't* be going to the mansion until the mission is complete.'

'Mission?'

'You won't,' she repeated, glancing at the window where the sun was still streaming in. 'And definitely not by day, when Lord Grailib could be a softy and listen to your mumbo-jumbo. Dusk is when he starts building to whatever he has to accomplish. Darkness is the Lord's strength. His powers are best by night. So after the mission –'

'What mission?' I yelled at the top of my voice to counter being unable to stamp my feet or throw my arms around.

In contrast, Conielle's voice became whispery. 'To wipe out Crickle Town.'

'W-wipe? *What do you mean?*'

Her tone was now teasing. 'Erase, scoop off – so as never to exist.'

I turned into pulp, picturing a whopping hollow in

the valley, where Crickle Town was. Nothing. Nobody. *Mum, oh, Mum. Don't let them take away my mum, no, don't*, I cried silently, hoping those forces above the clouds were hearing my wish. 'How insane! Why would he –'

'Got to be done before Humans bring down our homes to satisfy their greed. Now that you have found Trimoni's Pathway, the possibility of other Humans showing up here is very *real*. Getting rid of Crickle Town will rub out her Pathway forever.'

I raised my neck, attempting to sit, but the rope made certain I fell back flat. 'The humans in the valley no nothing about the Pathway, I'm not going to tell them. *I'm not!*'

'Believe you, *Bepa*?' Conielle jeered. 'Lord Grailib has to protect us from our enemy. That's his primary duty. So he will be working through the nights to make Crickle Town disappear. After that, I myself will take you to him. And though there won't be a Pathway for you to escape to the Valley of Humans –'

'Oh, no, I won't be able to even g-get back, oh, no.' My voice cracked into sobs, and I lay on the bed feeling dis-embodied.

'Soosh, soosh, no need to cry. You'll get used to us,' she cooed. 'The point is although you can't return to yack about the invisible woods to the Humans in the other valley towns, Lord Grailib will still throw you into his dungeons. He can't have you telling your tale to the rest of the Tree Folk either, can he?'

My wailing got louder.

Conielle silenced me with a cold stare. 'And what's best? Rin will never know of our cosy chat. Nor will he learn I was Miss Fifi, the Informer. And with Crickle Town gone, this mission will free us from Trimoni too.' She flung her arm with a flourish. 'A neat package – what more can I want?'

'You won't get away with this, you won't,' I growled.

'Mew!' Conielle replied, plainly scoffing at my empty threat. 'With Trimoni, Zylo and you out of the way, I will get Rin – well, I don't have time to stand around nattering with you all afternoon. Got an errand to run.'

'You can't leave me here while my hometown is being plucked off the Earth!' I bellowed.

Conielle lunged at me and a large blue cloth fell into her hands.

I was left on the bed my mouth out of action too.

Chapter 21

How long I'd remained gagged and tied to Conielle's bed, I didn't know. What was certain was the sun wasn't pushing through the window any longer. I gulped. It would soon be evening. Lord Grailib would start slipping into his almighty phase.

I had to stop the devastation facing Crickle Town; I had to rescue Zylo. But there was nothing I could do about either. If only I could warn Mum. I couldn't even call out to her just to keep me sane because my words got trapped behind Conielle's blue cloth.

I tried to shift. Arrgghh. If only I knew the magic for untying knots. My cheeks were soggy and my mouth limey. Was the rope severing my hands from my wrists? The pain was now barging into my mental agony. Biting,

biting. I shut my eyes and focussed on that pain ...

Suddenly, my wrists didn't feel stuck together; the ache just nibbled. My eyes popped open.

The rope had loosened around my wrists.

How? Quickly, I twisted my hands to get rid of that rope while my mind chased a bundle of thoughts. Maybe I'd inherited Trimoni's healing powers, the same way I had her protecting skills. Alolla did say I might possess more magic than I realised. What else could it be? My brain wasn't offering anything more plausible.

Great, my hands were free.

I untied the rope that held my upper body to the bed and sat up, yanking off the cloth around my mouth. Next, I unwrapped the rope which went down to my ankles and undid the knot that hinged me to the bottom of the bed. Then, a shake and a stretch, and I was dashing to the hallway.

I grabbed the handle of the front door and nearly kicked it. Damn, door magic. I then chased the windows and ended in a bedroom bigger than where I'd been. It had to be Conielle's. I darted to her window and gave it a shove. Bolted – like those in the other rooms. I scurried out, knocking down a little side table, and was about to step over what slid to the floor when I noticed it was a badge labelled *Lord's Circle Member*. With no time to think, I swept it up and put it in my pocket.

And then I was back in the hallway. Assuming I could get up to rooms with more windows, I gave the door in the tree trunk a try. That too wouldn't budge.

Creaking open now, though, was the front door.

Trembling, I crouched behind the hat stand, hoping Conielle wouldn't spot me behind the curtain of shawls.

The person who came in wasn't Conielle.

A short Tree-Folk man in a brown checked shirt was pushing a small cart full of boxes through the hallway and into the sweetshop. As soon as he disappeared in there, I sprang from my hiding place. I pounced at the front door that was shutting and got my foot in the doorway.

Back on the road, I remembered to breathe.

Phew!

Again, I glanced at Alolla's map. What if Conielle's road magic was still effective? The only way forward was to rely on passers-by at every turn.

Now the sun was going down; dusk was in front of my nose.

Chapter 22

I stood on Leaflog Street staring at the complex of trees that were joined together by fancy bridges to form the Lord's mansion. The trunks were taller and wider than the rest, making these mansion trees look like towers. Where was Lord Grailib? Which tower, er, tree was he in?

Each tree was manned by a guard with a Bluebark tree tattooed on his forehead. How was I going to get past? To keep a check on my nerves, I thrust my hands into my pockets. Hah, something I'd forgotten. Conielle's badge. Would it help? It was for esteemed Lord's Circle members after all. And the other good thing was, with photography not being a facet in the lives of the Tree Folk, the badge wasn't a photo ID that only Conielle could use.

Still, there was a hitch. Lord's Circle members were

bound to know their way around here. Traipsing from tree to tree asking for Lord Grailib was going to put the guards on alert. I gaped at the complex, quivering at the very might of it. It appeared as formidable as the Tower of London. Anne Boleyn had lost her head there. Was I going to lose mine?

Even the lights making the place a carnival site in the dusk couldn't warm the chill running through my spine. Every room in every tree was lit. Hold on – didn't Conielle say that darkness was the Lord's strength? My eyes instantly darted from window to window, playing *spot the unlit room.*

It was then that I saw a dark window in a tree at the centre of the complex. Surely it couldn't be more than a few magic words which brought on the lights each evening.

Why had only one room not bent to the call of magic?

My body went stiff remembering Zylo saying that the magic of the trees was strongest at the top. The dark window in the centre tree belonged to the topmost room.

Ooh, was that where Lord Grailib was making magic?

A surge of optimism conquered my dithers now that I had a thread to go by. I crossed the road and marched to the tree with the unlit window and said, 'I'm here to meet Lord Grailib.'

'Pass,' the guard said, barely moving his lips. Then I noticed him checking me over seemingly expecting to see something.

I drew Conielle's badge from my pocket, praying it was what he was referring to or that it would suffice as a *pass*. 'I forgot to clip it on,' I said, trying to keep my voice steady although my mind was drifting between dungeons and arrows.

The guard began mumbling.

Yeah! With shaky hands, I attached the badge to the top left side of my tee-shirt, ensuring it was well displayed now that I realised its value. Then I kept my eyes glued to the door which was increasing in size.

When that door opened, the guard stepped aside.

I entered the tree without asking for directions, so it would seem I knew the place; surely there'd be plenty of staff. But when I glanced around the circular hall, I didn't see a soul. Before I could turn back to the guard, the door shut behind me. I shuffled to the round room at the centre of the hall, wondering how I was going to get the door open with no magic. Just as I reached the room, though, the door opened, making me jump. Did the guard's door magic apply to this one too? Inside, I discovered yet another round room in the middle of the bigger one I was in. That room also had a door which opened when I got to it. I passed through several doors this way, going farther and farther into the trunk.

Finally, I was in a room with a difference. At the centre was a ring-shaped pit. It looked like the speak-o-port in Zylo's magic room. Maybe I had to get into it to talk with Lord Grailib. I dashed to the middle and down four steps to the pit. Before I knew what was happening, I shot upwards. I was travelling at the speed of a rocket in what could have been a lift with no walls or floor. With a jolt, I landed at the top of the tree trunk.

My feet found ground, and in front of me, there was a door which had to be to the dark room.

My heart in my throat, I watched that door open too. My knees buckled, but I shoved myself into the room, and a ray of light followed me and formed a spot beneath my feet when I paused. Then, picturing an old lord bent over a book of spells, I lunged to get to the darker part of the room. I couldn't move forward; it was like being re-strained by a viewless fence.

Coming towards me through a mass of cloud was a figure not less than seven feet tall.

When the man drew nearer, I saw Bluebark leaves hanging from a band around his head of long, dark tan-gled hair. The shoulder pads of his black leather-ish jacket too had bands and bands of leaves. I recalled Zylo claiming that Bluebark leaves brought prosperity and leadership.

The man stayed clear of the spotlight and hovered in the gloom, so I could barely see his face. Yet the aura he emitted made me feel mousy.

He was nothing like my mental image of an old, bent man.

'Lord Grailib?' I squeaked.

He waved his hand, either acknowledging his name, or signalling permission for me to speak. Or both.

'I, I'm here to ask you to release Zylo,' I stuttered. 'I don't think his family can handle losing another child.'

With a toss of his head, Lord Grailib discarded my plea just as Alolla and Rin had warned me he would. Then he pointed at the badge pinned to my tee-shirt. 'How did you get that?'

'It's Conielle's.'

'I see, I see. You are one of multiple talents. We meet at last.' Lord Grailib flashed me a grin that with even the limited visibility in the room I could see meant, *I know everything about you.*

My mind captured Conielle morphing into Miss Fifi. And I stood grimacing, while Lord Grailib shook his head slowly, clearly to keep me dangling.

'You are the trouble-making Miss Human who was

foolish enough to visit our invisible woods,' he said. 'The bad part of your folly is you will be close to Zylo. The good part is you will live in my supervised lock-up facility.'

'Is that what you call your *dungeons*?' I asked, unable to put a lid on my horror and disgust.

'I don't send children to the dungeons. But making the Tree Folk believe I do is the best way of getting them to ensure their brats don't get up to mischief.'

'You can't imprison humans!' I said.

'Can't, I?' Lord Grailib must have swelled, because his outline looked increasingly hulk-like. 'You're in my territory, I can do what I please.' His voice was also bloated. 'From the day I found out that that silly woman had created a Pathway to the Valley of Humans, I've feared it will be discovered. And it was, by you! Now I have no choice but to remove Crickle Town from the valley so that the Pathway will naturally disappear. Then we won't have any more unwanted guests crossing over. We aren't going to be displaced by Humans the way it happened in the past. Can't have history repeating itself, can we, *Missy*?'

The Missy-word put my brain into action. 'If your brand of magic can knock off a *whole* town, why couldn't it get rid of a group of humans who were felling your trees ages ago?' I chided.

'At the time, Grailib magic didn't have those types of powers. It took me years of magic-enhancement programs and learning to equip myself, for defence purposes, with the skill to root out towns.'

'Then why worry if townspeople from the valley *did* arrive?'

'Our philosophy is built on peace, not war.' Lord Grailib's hoity-toity tone had given way to earnestness. 'Destroying is not our goal. So much so, that I have disclosed my root-out ability to only the Lord's Circle members. We are doers of good magic. Using bad magic for anything is a last resort.'

I bit my lip, thinking of the protecting and possibly healing skills Trimoni and Trilata had given me. And, yeah, Alolla, who wasn't a Lord's Circle member, didn't seem aware that Crickle Town could be put in danger.

'Our laws prohibit creating a Pathway in order to prevent Humans from arriving here and placing us in a position that calls for bad magic,' Lord Grailib pressed on. 'The very foundation of our principles will crumble. Then we lose too. In the long run, nobody is a victor.' He pointed at me. 'So you see, by coming to the woods, you've done exactly what compels me to do bad magic!'

Like arrows, his words pierced my chest, making me reel. Crickle Town was about to go under – and all because of me. 'I *won't* tell any humans about the Pathway. I won't, I won't! I give you my word.'

'The word of a Human?' He snorted. 'I have been the Lord of Bluebark Woods for many years. My primary duty is to keep my citizens safe and protect our territory. Or else I won't be their Lord for long.'

'You'll be reducing heaps of human families to nothingness –'

'How sad.' Lord Grailib's voice was coated in sarcasm. 'Humans did the same to us when they cut down the trees we lived in. It's our turn to be the survivors.' He raised his arms above his head. 'Long live the Tree Folk of Bluebark Woods!'

Lord Grailib rushed through the dimness and into the light where I was. At last I could see his face.

Howling, I stumbled back several steps before locating my feet.

I'd seen this man before.

Chapter 23

I stared at the long, deep scar which spanned the length of Lord Grailib's left cheek and ended below his eye. I'd seen a scar of that magnitude only once before.

Like wild waves lashing the sea, a barrage of thoughts gushed into my mind and asserted my brain. 'Go on, then,' I said. 'If you think killing off Crickle Town is going to solve your problems, just do it!'

Lord Grailib clapped once as if he was saving his hands. 'My, my, aren't we brave?'

In spite of his cool-as-a-cucumber attitude, I was certain I was onto something. 'Do it,' I repeated. 'Then every person in Crickle Town will be gone.'

He looked startled.

'Yeah, *every* person.'

Lord Grailib's shoulders curved inwards and his chin pointed at the floor, turning him into a shorter man who had misplaced his uppity air.

Seeing the dramatic change in his demeanour, I knew I was pressing the right knobs. 'You will let Crickle Town remain forever, won't you?'

Lord Grailib went white. 'Why would I want to save Crickle Town? That's the very place I must get rid of to bury the Pathway.'

'That's *also* where you've got what is dearest to your heart.' I gave him a knowing nod.

He jerked at my gesture.

That gave me the fuel to follow my hunch. 'Your precious cargo, *remember*?'

Lord Grailib peered into my face, seemingly trying to suss out what I knew. I suppose he got his answers, because he raised his green eyes to the ceiling and shook his fists. 'I can't finish off the princess.'

'You mean the Princess of the Sky?'

'Sky! Sky! You met her? You know her?' His voice was hoarse.

'She's in my class, and she's my friend,' I claimed. 'Her mother died because of you.'

Lord Grailib fell to his knees. The whole seven feet of him. Then he bent over and banged his forehead on the floor. He was muttering what sounded like the sirens of torment.

He didn't appear to be someone who was gaining strength with sundown.

I stood rigid, watching him, but my head was rolling in what had led me to realise that Lord Grailib was Sky's missing dad. The towering man with green eyes and ears covered in the framed picture by her bedside – and of course his unmistakable scar which had stunned me then too. I recalled Sky saying that her dad didn't like being photographed. No wonder, when photography hadn't touched the lives of the Tree Folk; no wonder, when Lord Grailib needed to mask his identity. Then Alolla stating that he could without forming a Pathway go to the valley and her guessing he did, and her comment that he disappeared frequently long ago, but rarely left the woods later on – whereas Sky mentioned her dad wasn't around much but returned often for short visits, until he vanished for good.

Also, there was Sky's leaf scrapbook: the one she had complied with her dad. The leafy wallpaper her dad had put up in her bedroom ... Oh, yeah, just remembered, the leaf-shaped handle on her front door.

And here was a man seemingly obsessed with leaves.

Lord Grailib raised himself to his feet. Those slumped

shoulders seemed to be carrying the bulk of the woods. 'I have to maintain that, if no other way, I'd resort to bad magic to protect the woods because history still bites. History with the Humans.'

'And you almost had me fooled, and you certainly succeeded in fooling Conielle. But for how long? For here's your predicament: you can't erase Trimoni's Pathway by uprooting Crickle Town because living there you have a half-human child through your marriage to the *enemy*. So you can't fulfil your primary duty of keeping your citizens and territory safe. I'll tell your folk you have a conflict of interest. Then they'll see you're not fit to be the Lord of the Woods.'

Lord Grailib's face turned purple with rage. 'Take me for a fool? Didn't I tell you your fate? The doors of this mansion will remain shut till I transfer you to the lock-up. Your sentence is for *life*, Miss Human.' He was his seven feet again. 'That way, the Humans as well as the Tree Folk won't know there is a Pathway from the woods to the valley. Nor will the Tree Folk learn about my link to Humans, through Sky.' He rubbed his hands together, plainly displaying his pleasure of expelling all his fears with one solution.

The predicament was now mine.

It was also getting darker outside. And Lord Grailib's

might was clearly trending up and fuelling his determination to lock me away.

My stomach contracted into a ball. 'You don't deserve to be Lord of the Woods, because you broke the law too by separating Trimoni from her child,' I said, grabbing at whatever I could to put pressure on him before night set in.

His leaf clad shoulders shook with his sardonic laugh. 'If Alolla and Rin knew that a mother's right to her child was enshrined in our laws, they would have protested by now. The other Tree Folk, including the Lord Circle members, are unaware I banished Trimoni – when all this happened, I told Alolla and Rin to maintain I had sent her on a special assignment. I made them see that if the others knew Trimoni had created a Pathway to the Valley of Humans, they'd be furious with her for putting the woods in jeopardy.'

'But I came across that law in the *Laws of the Land* and told Alolla,' I said, pretending I'd been aware of the violation at the time. I scoffed down my lie and pushed on. 'So even if you lock me away to stop me from talking, Alolla will lodge a complaint.'

Lord Grailib's lip curled. 'She can't cause any real damage, unless she is willing to disclose Trimoni's wrongful act – the worst breach of law in the woods.'

'You are a smooth operator, aren't you Lord Grailib? By hiding what Trimoni did, especially, from the Lord's Circle members, you avoided being coaxed to root out Crickle Town. By suggesting to Alolla and Rin that the backlash will be against Trimoni, you got them also to remain quiet. You wanted to ensure your leadership wouldn't be threatened.'

'And it won't!' He stamped his foot, and the floorboards under my feet rattled.

But what made me shrivel was that I had run out of ideas.

Or had I?

'Here's what will be the end for you!' I said, my breath quickening as a thought plopped into my head. 'If I don't go back, Alolla and Rin will realise I wasn't able to persuade you to let Trimoni return to the woods – they'll see that even though creating a Pathway is the biggest breach of law here, that Trimoni will never be around to cop the blame. Then they would have nothing to lose. They'd also be angry at you for keeping Trimoni away. So, yeah. They're bound to tell the other Tree Folk there's a Pathway. *They'll* talk!' I sucked in what felt like all the air in the room. 'And if you are even thinking about tucking away Alolla and Rin in the dungeons, forget it. They go missing too, and your folk will get suspicious. They'll figure something was being *done* to that family, with Trimoni and now Zylo also gone.'

Lord Grailib stripped off the sneer on his face. He appeared to have done away with his voice too.

I stepped into the silence. 'With Alolla's disclosures, your sneaky way of handling what happened will come to light. The fact you concealed the possible danger to the woods won't go down well. You'll lose the trust of your Lord's Circle members and the rest of your folk. You'll be ousted if you don't root out Crickle Town. If you do, it will be the last of Sky!'

Lord Grailib came at me like a green-eyed monster. 'Go back, and stop Alolla and Rin from talking!' Now his voice was pounding with urgency. 'They can say nothing of the Pathway or of my banishing Trimoni.'

'Here's the deal,' I said, mimicking his reinvigorated tone of power. 'I know you won't wipe Crickle Town off the slate because of Sky – but you don't take revenge for what happened in the past by eliminating other human towns in the valley. You set Zylo free, and let Trimoni go back to her family. In return, other humans and Tree Folk will not hear about the Pathway. The Tree Folk won't know you infringed the law by separating Trimoni from Zylo. Most importantly, I won't tell your folk about your connection to humans through marrying Sky's mother and having Sky.'

'Can't have my folk losing faith.' Lord Grailib was wearing a distant look. 'They won't back me ... not this time ...'

I gathered he was referring to the commotion Alolla had told me about. Had I beaten the approaching night-fall and got him caving into what Conielle would have called my *mumbo-jumbo*?

I got my reply when he said, 'You've got a deal!'

I guzzled a cocktail of relief and cheer. 'There's one more condition,' I threw in. 'Conielle has to be tackled because her obsession with Rin is a threat to Zylo's family.'

Lord Grailib wrinkled his forehead and tugged at his chin. 'Well,' he said, emerging from his pondering. 'Given what's at stake, I'll have to make an exception and use bad magic to melt a seed in Conielle's memory: the seed that relates to Rin and his family – their past, their present. She won't remember anything regarding them.'

Then he surprised me with the brush strokes of gen-tleness in his voice. 'Oh, how I longed to see Sky. My princess. But it was risky to leave the woods, having been overthrown in the past while visiting the Valley of Humans. I couldn't let that happen again as the position of Lord has been held by my family for generations ...

You must bring Sky here.'

'B-but if Tree Folk can't spot what others of their kind have built – would Sky, being half-Tree Folk, see Trimoni's archway in my backyard wall in order to cross over to the woods, and also her Wall of the Mind in the woods to be able to return to the valley?'

'Tree Folk who have Human blood too like Sky will see Trimoni's creations, as long as they are travelling along her Pathway. But Sky must also wear a hat to cover her ears, we can't ignore the dangers. Apart from you, she is the only person who can know about that Pathway.'

'Got it,' I said. 'And I'll bring her.' Then, hearing feet, I spun to the door.

The footsteps belonged to Conielle.

I lunged backwards, just as Lord Grailib pointed at her with his long arm. He began mumbling a spell.

Conielle turned statue-still. When his muttering stopped, she burst out, 'My Lord, my badge has been stolen! Luckily, Edrit was on duty and let me in.'

With trembling fingers, I unpinned her badge from my tee-shirt and slipped it into my pocket.

'We have to catch the thief to stop unwarranted entry to the mansion ...' Conielle's voice trailed off as she suddenly saw me standing by. She swung back to Lord

Grailib. 'Oh, I didn't see you had a visitor.'

I gawped at Conielle. She didn't recognise me, not one bit. No wonder she didn't suspect me.

'I'll check on the theft right away,' Lord Grailib said. 'The Circle meeting is not until tomorrow. Is there anything else?'

'There *was* something.' Conielle narrowed her eyes. 'But I can't quite remember. Silly me.' She forked out a hyena giggle. 'I'll be at the meeting tomorrow. Sorry for barging in.'

Chapter 24

The next day, I didn't have to peep through the window of Zylo's tree house or knock on his door because Trimoni was mumbling the magic words of entry.

My heart sang a reunion song, watching the door expand and open.

We entered the trunk, and Trimoni stood beaming with her T pendant around her neck. Her outstretched arms were almost falling off.

Then there was Zylo doing a long jump to reach his mama, Alolla sobbing breathlessly, and Rin standing at ease with the sad slant to his mouth turned into a happy one.

Zylo couldn't seem to stop going, 'Mama ... Mama ... Mama ...'

Soon they were huddled together.

Then Zylo broke free from his family and dashed to me. 'Thanks, *sis*.'

The tree house shook with peals of laughter.

'Oh, well,' Trimoni said. 'You've got some of Trilata in you, so you *are* kind of sister to Zylo.'

'Guess I have acquired a whole other family, brother included.' I felt as wobbly as my voice. How blessed I was!

Then they were embracing me too.

'All this because of you,' Alolla said, hugging me tighter.

A man of few words, Rin said what he had to with his eyes.

I was clearly going to be their hero *forever*.

Finally, I got down to explaining the deal I had struck with Lord Grailib (except for the bit about Sky) and swore them to secrecy.

When I left the tree house, Zylo stepped out with me. He got an acorn from his pocket and threw it in the air. Then he watched it fall back into his palms and said, 'My lucky acorn.'

'Is that what you've been dipping into your pocket for?'

'I've been carrying this acorn around every day. Been sleeping with it under my pillow also, wishing for only one thing. I got it today.' He threw his skinny arms around me. 'You gave me a mama.'

Sky saw Trimoni's archway in my back wall.

'See what I said? The trick is to get into the backyard through my bedroom window.'

Sky was wearing a light blue pinafore dress and a hat which was trimmed with a crown of white fluffy flowers that resembled clouds. She looked the part: Princess of the Sky.

'Daddy,' she whispered, clutching her leaf scrapbook in one hand.

'Ready to cross over?' I asked.

Sky extended her other hand to me, and her palm felt wet in mine. Then we landed together on the other side.

Cloaked in black and striding towards us, along the strip of long grass I'd told him about, was Lord Grailib.

Sky flew into his arms crying, 'Daddy!'

And he swept her up as if she was featherweight. She was sobbing and tears were rolling down his cheeks too. They were transported to a place of their own with him every now and again mumbling, 'Princess of the Sky.'

The daughter of a lord, a leader – Sky's charisma didn't surprise me any longer. Didn't I say she was a natural?

Lord Grailib suddenly noticed me trying hard to blend into the background. He untangled his head from Sky's hair. 'Thank you for bringing my daughter to me. With her in my life,' he said, in a voice sizzling with joy, 'I have got back the heart I left behind in Crickle Town. Now I can listen to it and rule not just with my head.'

I stood tongue-tied; luckily, Sky's speech was intact.

'Marvel explained everything,' she said. 'But I want to live with *you*, Daddy.'

'Sorry, Princess, it's far too dicey.' He put Sky down gently. 'Besides, your mother's wish was that you grow up in the Valley of Humans. The least I can do for her is keep that promise.'

'Aunt Lucy is swell, but –'

'Lucy is a wonderful woman. She was the only person who didn't dance around the edges trying to find a story for your mother's sudden marriage. She is sensible, kind. You are in safe hands.' Lord Grailib had a twinkle in his eye. 'Now that you know where I am and how to get here, you can visit me any time. Mind you always wear a hat!'

'I knew it, I knew it, I knew I was making things happen,' Sky said, waving the scrapbook at Lord Grailib as though it had to do with her claim. 'The best was when I first observed that with my mind I could bring

Mummy out of the doldrums she slipped into whenever you left. She used to drop her weep and become almost happy at least for a while. That allowed her to cope. Of course, in the longer term her sadness prevailed. Then I tried it on Aunt Lucy when Buster, her dog, died. Her behaviour followed a similar pattern.'

'You seem to have the magic of instilling happiness,' Lord Grailib said. 'Your grandfather had that special skill.'

Sky drew a loud breath. 'That's how I got it! I started using that skill at school also. It seemed to work better with the kids, as the ones I tried it on became all bubbly. Maybe they weren't struggling with anything specifically sad, unlike Mummy and Aunt Lucy, so happiness might have got to them in a bigger dose. I wanted to surround myself with friends, Daddy, because I felt lonely when you left. I thought if Mummy and Aunt Lucy didn't figure that *something* was causing their sudden change of mood, the kids at school wouldn't either.'

I recalled Ava saying that the others seemed to be happy around Sky.

'Being my daughter, you must have covert skills,' Lord Grailib said. 'The ability to do magic from a distance – no touching, tapping or chanting spells aloud.'

I chewed my lip. Lucky Sky. If I could also do magic

without drawing attention, I wouldn't be labelled *weird* or *freaky*.

If only ...

'Then why when you disappeared from our lives completely, did my, erm, magic stop working on Mummy?' Sky asked, interrupting my wishful thoughts.

'You need training to hone your skills. I will coach you myself, Princess.' Lord Grailib squinted at me. 'I heard you were being bullied in school for using magic openly.'

Miss Fifi! Did Conielle have to blab about everything? 'Yeah,' I said, staring at the floor, pretending to be searching for my feet.

'You may also have a layer of covert skills lying dormant inside you,' he said.

I grabbed my throat. 'Me?'

'Those abilities might surface with coaching,' Lord Grailib went on. 'I will give Trimoni permission to train you in magic.'

'*You will?*' Oh, my gosh, he *was* consulting his heart. 'And could that mean nobody around me would know I'm foreseeing and preventing accidents?'

Lord Grailib chuckled. 'That's how it could be.'

My head went quiet. Was it a preview of what lay ahead? The Tune had ceased playing for me since I'd discovered how it came about. Maybe this training would put an end to the whispers and giggles, and clear them from my head too. This inner silence was new to me: I wanted to stay there; oh, how I wanted to stay there. Yet I scooped my voice out of the lull. 'Thank you, thank you, *thank you*, sir!'

I raced across my backyard with my feet barely touching the ground. Then a glimpse of Mum at the kitchen sink, made me pause and shut my eyes. I held my arms plane-like and twirled; I wasn't wishing, I tell you, because if I were my hands would have been clenched. What was making me spin like a top was that I didn't weigh with hoping and wanting.

'Thank you for sparing Crickle Town and letting me hang onto Mum,' I said to those forces above the clouds, 'and for granting Zylo and Sky their wishes.'

Then I was spinning the other way. Again, my hands weren't clenched. 'Thank you,' I said, 'for leading me to a place that could train me to do magic wearing a *normal* badge.'

Back in my bedroom, Kango and I browsed through my Baby Book – yeah, I'd grown fond of it – until we were jolted by a tap on my window.

Sky was peeking into my room, starry-eyed and all.

I opened the window and helped her in.

'It was magic,' she said, and we doubled over laughing. 'Imagine discovering I'm like 50 percent Tree Folk!'

'It had to be an Everest for you to gobble, when I told you. Learning there was "a bit of Tree Folk" in me,' I said, quoting Zylo's words, 'was mountainous enough at first.'

'Now that I've met Daddy, it feels swell. A good thing I got Mummy's ears though!'

We both doubled over again.

'And the magic, the magic! That Wall of the Mind was tops! But, hey, thank you for getting back Daddy for me ... The way I've treated you – I'm sorry.' Sky bit her lip. 'The first day you insisted on fields that were not there, I got an odd vibe I had never picked up in anyone else. Then when you started saving people beyond your range of vision, I suspected you had *moments*, because I had too.'

I gulped reflecting on Sky's puzzling behaviour and the mysterious looks she'd been giving me. Now I knew why.

'I never mentioned my *moments*,' Sky continued, 'as I didn't want Mummy to work out I was curing her, sort of. I was also scared I might be sent off to a shrink or whatever.'

'You're lucky you can do magic unnoticed,' I said.

'Except when I used the newer skill I picked up, it was you who took the rap.'

'*Me?*'

'I was puzzled at first and fooled around with that skill at home but never at school,' Sky said. 'Shifting stuff around the class –'

'You! Well, now that I know your father is magical, it figures,' I said, hotting up.

'I was terrified of being caught out and having the others call me names. They respected me. I was the most popular girl in the class. How could I spoil that? Then when I realised they were starting to regard you as odd, I thought if they spotted the moving objects, they'd think it was you.'

My ears went pop listening to her. *How could she?*

Sky was wearing a beetroot face. 'I felt mean, but convinced myself that pinning the freakiness to you was okay as you were using your skills openly, and it didn't seem to bother you. Knew nothing about the covert-skill stuff which you didn't have. I was dying to try my latest ability at school. Of course, I didn't want to get you into trouble – that's why I focused my mind on just a pen. When it moved but appeared to go unobserved, I got excited and attempted to shift Mandy's files. I left you to take the teasing.' Her voice shook. 'It was h-horrible of me. Horrible!'

'Still,' I said, my memory serving to hose down the

froth inside me. 'You didn't dob on me about the missing arch. My first day at Crickle Town Primary would have been gross if everyone poked fun at me. After the bullying I faced at my old school, I was frantic. And the day I rang the fire bell you stood up for me in front of the whole school.'

'I didn't want busybodies like Bea to get at you. The thing is you made your *moments* obvious. And as I said, I didn't know about covert skills, so I was furious with you. Even decided not to introduce you to my gang.'

'Oh?' I pricked up my ears.

'My gang's swell, but if they laughed at you, I would have been torn. Knowing I felt a connection to your *moments*, not sticking up for you would have also been lousy. On the other hand, if I took your side, it could have led to cracks in my gang. I didn't want to take the risk – it was selfish of me.'

My memory again retrieved one of Ava's comments, the one about Sky's gang being called the Happy Campers because they didn't squabble. 'It's okay,' I said, struggling to feel so.

'You're not selfish like me,' Sky said. 'Most people would have ditched the rescue effort if they were being ridiculed. You never let others come to harm. You put them before yourself. You don't need to do happiness-instilling magic to make you seem good – you are just plain *good*. A hero, really.'

Again I was warmed by a glow in my heart.

But while Sky coughed nervously, I swallowed a dollop of guilt at how I'd considered leaving Ava to fend for herself, coming to my senses only just in time to save her. We all had our instances of weakness. So what right did I have to condemn Sky? And, yeah, I believed she didn't like mocking others; she had proved that to me.

'Bet it's too late to invite you to join my gang?' Sky asked.

'*Join?* For real?'

'Real.'

'Unreal!' I said.

Sky was all smiles. 'We will have the induction to-morrow in the presence of Mandy, Ellie and Clare – you'll like them. Then, you are officially in!'

My mind, spirit and body too, I think, soared. I was going to belong to a gang. Yeah, me. That's right. How cool was that?

'Hey,' Sky said, bringing me back to ground level. 'I've got a plan: until your training equips you with covert skills to protect others from a distance, I'll squirt happiness on the bullies who begin reacting in a mean way during your *moments*. If they're happy, bet they'll forget to be mean.'

'Thanks!' I said, raising my thumbs. 'I guess even the Bea-types of this world can't be happy and mean at the same time.'

After Sky left, Kango and I peeped out of my window and gazed across the yard at the footpath to the magical Tree Folk. 'I'm not a witch, not a fairy,' I said. 'I'm an ordinary kid with an *extra* attached. And I love being extraordinary.'

I tell you, that's why my name is Marvel.

Please Review this Book

Thank you for reading *Not a Witch, Not a Fairy*. If you enjoyed it, please consider leaving a review wherever you bought the book.

Your support is truly appreciated. Thanks in advance.

Best wishes,
Navita Dello

Other Books by Navita Dello

The Secret of the Ballet Book

Sierra cannot believe her luck when a dancer steps out of her ballet book and offers to train her for the audition that might spare her from having to quit ballet. However, unless the dancer forever re-enters the page within the deadline set by the witch who trapped her, she is fated to disappear. Would Sierra succeed not only at the audition but also at getting the dancer out of the book for good? Or would Sierra end up inside the ballet book too? Worse still, disappear?

Mimi-Marina and the Magical Doll Shop

School rules, home rules, Mimi-Marina is up to her neck with rules. So, for the school holidays, she is glad to help out at her mum's seemingly rule-free Global Village Doll Shop. She soon feels a magical vibe in the shop and makes a discovery which ties her down to freaky rules that get her into trouble, bringing the shop to a stand-still. To get the shop back on track, she must go to the Realm of Dolls. But going to the Doll Realm is fraught with danger for her. Would her life change forever? Even worse, might she never return home?

Made in the USA
Middletown, DE
16 July 2018